WITCH OR WITHOUT YOU

THE WITCHES OF HOLIDAY HILLS COZY MYSTERIES

CAROLYN RIDDER ASPENSON

MAGNUM GRACE PUBLISHING

Copyright © 2023 by Carolyn Ridder Aspenson

All rights reserved.

No part of this book may be reproduced in any form or by any electronic or mechanical means, including information storage and retrieval systems, without written permission from the author, except for the use of brief quotations in a book review.

Cover Design: Vila Design

For my parents
RIP

1

The crowd at the Enchanted Bookstore and Café overflowed onto the sidewalk. Several of the customers held to-go cups in their hand but had stuck around to chat. Holiday Hills wasn't the biggest small town in the North Georgia Mountains, but it offered tourists a bird's-eye view of what it would have been like to live in a Hallmark movie. Quaint and unique boutiques lined our main street. People drove in from Atlanta to buy candles at the candle shop. The owner, an ornery old witch who hated change, refused to move with the times and get a cell phone, let alone a website. The Atlanta crowd didn't care. They received her candle sale schedule every month and made a day of it, stopping at the Enchanted for a cup of coffee and a pastry while they waited for the stores to open.

Normally, I'd use the back entrance, but I'd heard the crowd outside from my apartment above and decided to see what the fuss was all about. Strange things had happened in the past, and I'd learned to have a watchful eye. Holiday Hills was different. Magical beings lived among humans.

Magic happened daily, and sometimes I was the one responsible.

Humans didn't know about the magicals, and except for a glitch in the matrix every now and again, they saw a different version of reality when magic happened. It made for interesting conversations, for sure.

An older warlock, Mr. Hastings, or Waylon, as he'd preferred to be called, walked into the Enchanted along with me. He and Bessie Frone, also a witch, the store owner, and my deceased mother's best friend, had been inching toward a romantic relationship for a few months. They'd yet to say it was official, but everyone figured it was. When two people hold hands and smooch, as Bessie called it, in public, it was official.

If I hadn't cast a spell to check, I would have said someone cast a love spell on Waylon because the once cranky old coot had transformed into a kind-hearted man, and honestly, I was just getting used to him that way.

Cooper, my Burmese cat and familiar, bolted in and rushed to the kitchen. Waylon nearly tripped over him as he passed. My cat skidded into the swinging door and hit it with a thud. His strong body propelled right through, and the door swung closed.

I glanced at Waylon, waiting for a nasty comment to leave his lips because that had been Waylon's nature for years, but he didn't say anything. He just laughed. Since I knew there was no love spell, Bessie's sweet and loving personality had impacted Waylon in a positive way. If I wasn't a witch and didn't believe in magic, that would have done it for me.

The sudden change in personality didn't stop me from protecting my family. I'd told Waylon if he was good to

Bessie, he was okay in my book, but one step in the wrong direction, and I'd turn that old warlock into a frog.

And he knew I wasn't exaggerating.

I followed Cooper into the kitchen and scooped him up from the top of the metal counter and set him on the floor. "You just ate."

Bessie narrowed her eyes at my familiar. "Did he now? He said he was starving."

"I am starving. She only fed me one can of tuna. I'm a two-can-a-morning, one-can-at-lunch, and two-at-night cat. The women outside waiting for the candle shop to open, can hear my stomach roaring."

"Oh, the drama," I said.

He climbed back onto the counter. "You want me to be strong to protect you, right?" He scooted close to the edge near where Bessie stood and rubbed his face against her side.

The little booger could manipulate even the strongest of witches.

Bessie tilted her head to the side. "He's got a point."

Warlock and chief of police, Remmington Sterling, sauntered through the kitchen door. He'd dressed in full uniform and looked like the chief of police that he was. A soft ping zipped through my heart. It was small, but I noticed it. Too bad I couldn't determine if that was a romantic ping or a guilt-about-my-ex-boyfriend ping. The pings pinged like twin Ping-Pong balls, hitting my heart and my head quick and hard, and I had trouble deciphering my feelings. Romance and guilt were sometimes similar feelings. They both screwed with my head.

My life was complicated.

"I checked into the information you received," he said. He stuffed his hand into his pocket and removed a plastic-wrapped toothpick. After unwrapping it and sticking it in his mouth, he asked, "Can we discuss it privately?"

"I'll stay here and eat," Cooper said. "Call me if you need me."

"Yes, sir," I said with sarcasm.

I pointed at Bessie. "One can. No more, please."

"Yes, ma'am," she said.

Mr. Charming, our resident green parrot and Bessie's familiar, had been perched on the edge of a bookcase in the center aisle of the book section. He flew over as I extended my arm out for him. "Abby loves Mr. Charming. Abby loves Mr. Charming," he said.

"Yes, she does," I said. "So, what's going on?" I asked Remmington.

Mr. Charming hopped off my arm and wobbled to his multistemmed perch near the counter. He made himself comfortable on the top stem.

"There's no known mission in the North Georgia Mountains or anywhere in Georgia. The closest active mission with the bureau is in Tennessee. They won't confirm or deny that Gabe is there."

Gabe, the ex-boyfriend, was also a warlock, and the previous chief of police in Holiday Hills. My best friend, Stella, a human, said I had a thing for police chiefs. I hadn't looked at it that way, but she was right. Except my thing for Gabe had been love, and my thing for Remmington was mostly just confusing.

"Of course, they won't." I bit my bottom lip. Discussing your ex-boyfriend's situation and your desire to help him with your current, well, interest, wasn't easy, but it was necessary, and thankfully, Remmington was willing to help. I worried the whole *nice guys finish last* theory would eventually apply to him when Gabe returned, but I couldn't promise anything. And by that, I meant I couldn't promise if Gabe would return, or if I'd stay with Remmington.

Six months before, I'd had strange dreams about a crazy-haired, dirty man with long, scraggly hair and an equally long, scraggly beard to match, wearing a clown nose. He did nothing but say, *Gabe's not coming home* over and over. Gabe had been sent on a secret mission with the Magical Bureau of Investigations, and when he learned—from me—that the *mountain man* had entered my dreams, he cast a spell to make me fall out of love with him.

Did it work? Eh, I'd say fifty-fifty. I wasn't sure how I felt about Gabe, and things were a big hot mess since I'd been seeing Remmington. I liked Remmington, and yes, I had feelings for him, but was it love? I didn't know, but it didn't feel like love. I couldn't bring myself to think about it until I resolved things with Gabe, and to do that, I had to find him.

I knew the mountain man was out to get him, for reasons unclear to me, so I'd resolved myself to the fact that I'd have to either get to Gabe first or find the mountain man, let him lead me to Gabe, and then make sure he paid for his crimes. All of which had been impossible in those six months. When you're flying by the seat of your pants, whether on a broom or not, finding a needle in a haystack was virtually impossible. Gabe was that needle in the haystack. The problem was, since no one knew where Gabe was, I worried something awful must have happened to him, something awful that included the strange mountain man. I'd never forgive myself if I didn't do something.

"What do you want to do next?" he asked.

"I don't know, but I've asked too much of you already. You've been patient and understanding, and I really appreciate it, but this is my thing, not yours, and it's awkward."

"It's not awkward."

I dipped my head down and looked up at him. "Liar."

"Okay, it's a little awkward, but I wouldn't offer to help if I didn't want to."

I kissed him on the cheek. "Thank you." I'd had to look up at him to kiss him. At nearly six feet tall, I towered over most men, but not Remmington. Thank Goddess.

Not Gabe, either. I shook off the mental image of him floating through my mind. I had things to do, work things, witchy things, laundry even. I didn't have time to miss Gabe or analyze my relationship with Remmington.

My best friend, Stella, a human, stormed through the entrance. "Hey, you two love birds." She waved her hands. "No PDAs in the Enchanted. You know the rules!" She set her laptop bag next to mine on the table I'd always used as a makeshift desk.

Remmington's lips curved upward.

I blushed. "We're not publicly displaying any affection. He's got a toothpick in his mouth. We're just having a conversation."

"Mm-hmm," she said. "Saved by the toothpick. Again." She poked him in the arm. "You sure love those things, don't you?"

"I've got to get to work," Remmington said. "I'm interviewing a woman for the new K-9 position. She's got a German Shepherd. Word is he's a tough dog, too."

"Aren't all German Shepherds?" I asked.

"I've known a few who failed K-9 school. If I hear anything, I'll let you know."

"Thanks."

Cooper sauntered out of the kitchen and over to the table. I'd already dropped my bag there earlier and began setting up my laptop. "So," I said to Stella. "Big plans today?"

"I'm editing a romance." She cringed.

"You sound like you hate romances."

"I don't hate them, but after reading so many, they all sound the same. Woman's heart is broken. She meets a new man she can't stand. They fall in love. Blah, blah, blah. I'm itching for a good serial killer plot. You know, the chop 'em up and spit 'em out stuff."

"Sounds lovely."

She laughed. "What about you? Are you still thinking about Gabe and what's going on with him?"

There were times I wished Stella was a magical. Not being able to share things with her was hard, and I hated leaving her out of such an important part of my life. I knew how it felt. As a child, my mother had bound my powers, so even I knew nothing about the magicals. When she died, the binding spell died with her, and poof! My witchiness showed up like the least liked cousin at the family reunion. Talk about a shock. At first, I had no control over my powers, and every time my nose itched, magic happened. Yes, my means of casting magic was through a rub of my nose, which wasn't at all attractive. As time passed though, my gift grew, and I'd learned to channel it into my hands instead of my nose. I thanked Goddess for that daily.

But those first few weeks as a witch, coupled with mourning the loss of my mother, were crazy. Cooper, who'd just been my cat before, started talking to me, in English, and it all went downhill from there. Not really. In truth, I loved being a witch. It was the trials and tribulations that came with it I didn't like. Because of all that, I couldn't share the truth with Stella. It went against magical code, and if I did, I would suffer a fate I didn't want to imagine. So, instead, Stella believed Gabe had dumped me, which he basically had, and was on a special assignment for the Georgia Bureau of Investigations.

She tapped her pencil on the table and waved her hand in my face. "Hello? You there?"

I cleared my thoughts with a head shake. "I'm trying not to think about Gabe, but it's not easy."

She eyed the notebook I'd just removed from my bag. "Is that the book you're working on for the publisher, or another one?"

"What makes you think I have another one I'm working on?"

She raised her eyebrows. "So that's how we're doing this? Okay. I know you're working on another book because you're my best friend, and I can practically read your mind. You've been taking notes in that thing for months now. I'm pretty sure since Gabe ended things. If I had to guess, I'd say it's about a young witch who solves the mystery of a murdered chief of police." She leaned back in the chair and folded her arms over her chest. "Am I close?"

Stella got me. "Close. Yes, it's a new idea about a young witch, but she's not investigating a murder. She's investigating a missing person."

"Interesting."

"You don't know the half of it," Cooper said from under the table.

I nudged him with my foot even though Stella simply heard meows.

"You don't know. You don't know," Mr. Charming repeated from his perch.

Stella narrowed her eyes at the parrot, then leaned in close and whispered, "Sometimes the bird creeps me out. Like, where did that come from? You don't know? Did he just suddenly pull it out of his feet or something? I feel like he understands what we're saying and knows stuff we don't."

"Of course, he does." I played into her fear for giggles. "He's from another reality, and he's here to protect us."

She laughed. "I'd rather have your chunk of a cat protect me. Not that he could do much, but at least he wouldn't creep me out."

Cooper climbed onto a chair and peeped his small, brown head over the tabletop. "Did she just call me fat?"

"Aw, see?" Stella patted him on the head. "He knew I was complimenting him. He's thanking me."

Cooper sneezed on her.

"Ew!"

I laughed. "That was for calling him fat," I said.

"I didn't call him fat."

I cringed. "You kind of did."

"Even so, how would he know?"

"The bird told him." I couldn't stop myself from laughing.

2

Writing paranormal cozy mysteries was a full-time job with no specific hours. I knew muses were real, but either I didn't have one or she'd run away. Most writers claimed to write when their muse inspired them, but I wrote to pay my bills and eat, so I made it an almost daily thing.

Lately, that hadn't been the case, but prior to my mother's death, and before I'd known I was a witch, I'd spent most of my free time writing. Stella would have said I lacked a life other than pizza and Hallmark movie nights with her, and she would have been right. But in my defense, I'd moved home after my husband cheated on and divorced me, so I needed the time to deal with that.

Finding out about my witchy ways was, in retrospect, challenging to my writing career, but it had been entertaining, and once I accepted and understood my destiny, I rocked it.

And I'd been rocking it ever since.

That writing career? I was lucky to have continued to do

well, finally branching out from being a ghost writer for a USA Today Bestselling author who didn't deserve the status, to writing under my own name and achieving the same success.

Admittedly, I'd tried to have a life, and I did for a while, while dating Gabe. And now I was with Remmington.

Life was complicated, but I'd figure it out. I always did. The problem was, I'd overestimated my capabilities, and the deadline for my newest book loomed over me like a rain cloud. I was 30,000 words into a book with a minimum requirement of 55,000 words, and it had me completely stumped. In my latest, I had created a world where the main character, also a witch, only older than my thirty-ish years, needed to rescue her friend from an unknown force. They always said, write what you know, so I did, but with a twist. I didn't know who *they* were, but I did what they said anyway. It was possible the only way to finish my book was to find Gabe. I would have calculated the words per day I'd need to write to finish in time after Gabe had been rescued, but I had no clue how long it would take or if I would succeed in that rescue attempt. Some witches flew by a broom, but not me. I flew by the seat of my pants in both my career and personal life.

I might have had writers block in that moment, but I didn't have *find Gabe* block. So, I bid my bestie farewell, grabbed my things, including my cat, and headed back up to my apartment.

I attempted another effort with my locating crystal using a world map I'd found in my mother's things. If Gabe was locatable on solid ground, the crystal would know. If he was outside of this reality or somehow not touching earth, the crystal could be useless. Of course, he could have cast a blocking spell over himself, but I had hoped he wouldn't do that. Previous attempts to locate him had me thinking he was in a place no magic could reach. But I realized, if the mountain man and his posse had Gabe, and knew I'd looked for him, they'd put him where the crystals couldn't find him, land bound or otherwise. Even if Gabe was suspended in the air, the crystal's power would be stopped. If that was the case, I couldn't locate him with it, and I'd just have to work harder.

And the only way to do that was through the magical dark web.

Cooper lay on the back of the couch, staring at my fingers tapping away on my laptop. "You sure you want to do this?"

"Yes."

"I'm getting a strong sensation telling me to make you let this go."

"Tell the being sending that sensation you're not the boss of me, and frankly, neither are they."

"Abby, there are rules."

"Rules are meant to be broken." I clicked on a link to a magical site known for locating hard-to-find items. I'd resisted in the past, thinking it wouldn't work because Gabe wasn't an item, but I had no other choice.

"No. Not that one. You know there are ramifications for that."

I flipped around and met Cooper eye to eye. "Gabe needs me. He wouldn't have cast that spell over me if he didn't think the situation was dangerous. I can't just let him do that. If the universe or the powers that be wanted that, they would have made the spell work for more than a hot minute. But look at me. I'm here, desperate to help him. Now, that's what I'd call a strong sensation."

Cooper sighed. "I'd just like to say I am not in agreement with your actions." He crawled off the back of the couch and curled up in the chair beside it, his face buried into the chair's back.

"Understood." I filled out the information requested on the link and hit send. Then I waited. If the dark web had something for me, it would show up sooner rather than later.

I stared at a photo of my mother hanging on the wall, then surveyed the rest of my home. If someone were to describe my apartment, they'd use words like shoebox, cramped, cute, teeny. I loved my apartment. It smelled like lavender and vanilla, soothed my soul, and was my safe place. A buzzing sound filled my ears. I instantly felt a humming vibration in the room. The energy grew stronger by the second. "Oh, something's happening."

"Yeah, something's happening all right." Cooper lifted his head and glanced around. He climbed off the chair and stood in the doorway to my bedroom. "And it's hot and negative."

"It's not negative. It's intense. There's a difference."

The vibration's hum grew louder. The lavender and vanilla scents vanished, replaced by a strange spicey smell I couldn't place. Maybe some kind of cheap aftershave? My stomach tensed. I set my laptop back on the coffee table and closed the screen. The humming buzzed so strongly, my laptop moved an inch on the table. The few lights I'd had on blinked on and off, finally settling on off. The hum had deepened, causing everything in my apartment to shift. The furniture slid on the carpet, and candles I'd placed throughout my small family room area toppled onto the ground. Thankfully, none of them were lit.

"Oh, boy," Cooper said. He stood on his hind legs and

drew his front ones close to his chest as if he planned to punch the vibration. "I'm ready!" He hopped first on one foot and then the other. "I'm definitely ready." He hissed several times.

Lightning flashed. *Don't Stop Believin'* blared from my Amazon Echo. I flicked my wrist and turned it off. It switched back on. "Oh, for the love of Goddess. Enough!" I encased Cooper and I in a secure protective circle, then raised my arms and screamed, "Show yourself!"

The vibration increased as a shadow dropped from beyond my ceiling down onto my floor. Cooper stood at the edge of the protective circle as it morphed and shaped into something other than a blob. After only seconds, a male human-like figure appeared. "Your request has been denied." His voice was deep like thunder. "Drop this nonsense immediately, or there will be consequences."

Cooper whipped his head around and stared at me with eyes the size of saucers. "What the heck is that?"

"Don't ask me!" I made eye contact with the being. "Why? Who are you anyway?"

"Oh, great," Cooper said. "I'm going to have to save you from some submagical mutation with superpowers. And I haven't had a snack yet. Great."

The being's energy shifted from a deep black to a soft gray, then slowly mutated into a glowing crystalized white. He stepped closer. Cooper hissed. I wasn't afraid. He'd humanized himself enough for me to feel comfortable. Besides, I was a tough witch. He didn't scare me.

Much.

"I am Kaedan. I have been sent from the mighty to deny your request for assistance in locating your warlock."

"He's not my warlock. He's an investigator for the

Magical Bureau of Investigations, and I think he's in trouble."

"His mission is not your concern."

"Fine. It's not my concern. Tell me if he's okay and safe from the mountain man, and I'll drop this."

"I am not authorized to discuss top security information. You must trust what I tell you. Involving yourself will endanger you, the people you care about, and the warlock you wish to help."

"What about the mountain man? He's threatened me. Can you do something about him?" I asked.

"We are aware of the situation."

"Great. What does 'aware of the situation' mean exactly?"

Kaedan showed no emotion and spoke like an alien on an early season of the original *Star Trek*. He kept his arms against his sides. His eyebrows didn't move. His lip didn't twitch. His breathing stayed steady. He did not give a witch's broom about what I wanted. "You have been warned. Failure to comply will be met with severe consequences."

I stepped over the protective circle's line and broke the spell. "Oh, yeah?"

"Oh, crap," Cooper said.

"Do me a favor, Kaedan. Go back to the mighty and tell them they can stuff it." I flicked my wrist, and Cooper and I disappeared.

We landed in the Enchanted surrounded by shelves filled with books. Thankfully, the café was closed. "He thinks he can scare me?"

Cooper pushed against my leg. "Uh, Ab?"

I glanced down at him. He jerked his head toward the pair of large black boots on the other side of the bookshelf. "Oh."

Kaedan walked around the shelf and stood in front of us. He smiled down at me, which, given my nearly six-foot height, was impressive. "I do not mean to anger you. I merely come to inform you. You cannot fight someone else's battles. You may feel it necessary, but I assure you, it is dangerous."

"I'm not trying to fight anyone's battles. I'm trying to find someone."

"I understand your actions. In attempting to locate the warlock, however, you will locate the being you call the mountain man as well. That is not your battle."

"The thing haunted my dreams, and he showed up in a fun house! It is my battle."

Cooper rubbed against my leg.

Kaedan's eyes softened. Had I earned some compassion? "Gabe must fight this battle on his own."

"Can you guarantee he'll win?"

He shook his head.

"Then I'm not stopping."

"Please. We cannot guarantee your safety."

I tilted my head. "Wait a minute. You don't know what or who the mountain man is, do you? Your mighty-whatever-powers-that-be people are stumped, aren't they?"

His eyes shifted from the left to the right. His Adam's apple bobbed up and down.

"I'm right, aren't I? Just say it."

"I am not at liberty to discuss such matters." He dipped his head down, glanced up at me again and gave a miniscule nod. Just one. Barely noticeable. I wasn't even sure it was what I thought it was. Was he saying I was right?

I raised my eyebrow and nodded once to check.

He gave me the slightest of nods again.

"Great," Cooper said.

I cleared my throat. "Fine. I'll stay out of it."

Kaedan disappeared.

"What the—" Cooper asked.

"I think he just told me to go for it."

3

I transported us back to my apartment and fed Coop a can of tuna. He'd need the energy for the coming days. Who was I kidding? He'd need the energy to make it to bedtime.

"What do we do now?" he asked.

"We wait until you're done eating to discuss it."

"Why?" A piece of tuna dropped onto his chest. "Oh, that's why, isn't it?"

I cringed. "Yes."

The clock read half past two. I'd yet to sleep, having spent the entire day focused on Gabe. I leaned against my small kitchen counter and thought things through as Cooper ate. The knock on my door jarred me back to reality. "It's the middle of the night."

"Don't answer it. It can't be good."

"They wouldn't knock if it was someone bad."

"Good point, but still."

I walked the few steps to the door, checked through the peephole and then whispered back to Cooper. "It's Kaedan. Why is he knocking instead of appearing in here? What should I do?"

"Dead bolt the door."

"I'm opening it."

"Of course you are." He walked over and stood in front of me.

I swung the door open. "What?" Something was different about him. His hair, maybe? Had he changed clothing? No. It was neither. It was his energy. His energy felt different. "Are you ill?"

"May I come in, please?"

I pushed the door farther. "Be my guest. Forgive the mess. Oh, wait. You caused it."

Cooper hissed.

Kaedan walked in and stood in front of the couch. Without moving or speaking, everything shifted back to where it belonged. How had he done that? Most magic required a movement to make something happen. A blink of an eye, even the act of swallowing. Just something. Magicals couldn't just will magic to happen. It needed movement or a spell. But Kaedan could. Why? I decided to wait until I could trust him more to ask. If I could ever trust him. In the meantime, I'd watch and be careful. Trusting someone or something had done me wrong before, and I wouldn't let that happen again. "Thank you," I said.

He smiled.

"Why are you here?"

He stuck his hand in his pants pocket and removed a pack of gum. He opened a piece and popped it in his mouth like we were just hanging out, chatting. "I know Gabe." He held out the pack. "Would you like a piece? It's cinnamon."

"No. I don't like cinnamon. And you know Gabe? How?"

"We worked together a long time ago. A pretty intense

mission. A witch went missing, and we were assigned to find her. Unfortunately, when we did, she was no longer alive."

"Oh, I'm sorry. I didn't know."

"The witch was an MBI agent as well. It was complicated."

"Did you know her?"

"She was my partner. She was involved in a deep undercover investigation that led us to a secret MBI agent. He killed her, and he's paying for his crimes."

"Oh, I'm so sorry."

"What's done is done. I've been assigned to keep you from tracking Gabe."

"Assigned? Would babysit be a better word?"

"In layman's terms, yes," he said.

"I don't need a babysitter."

"I don't believe you do either, which is why I would like to make you an offer."

I crossed my arms over my chest and hitched out my left hip. "What kind of offer?"

"Let me find Gabe for you."

My arms fell to my sides. "Why would you do that, and how can I trust you?"

He held out his hand, and a photo appeared. He handed it to me. I gasped when I saw the photo of Gabe and I facing each other and holding hands. His smile sent a familiar vibration surging through my body. We were happy. In love. I remembered the feelings swirling around us that day. "Where did you get this?"

"Turn it over."

I flipped the photo over slowly. Written in Gabe's handwriting was, *If something happens to me, take care of her.* I swallowed back a lump forming in my throat. "Did he give this to you?"

"And from my view, the only way to take care of you is to find Gabe."

"I don't understand."

"If I don't, you will, and I can't let anything happen to you. I made a promise to my friend, and I won't let him down. So, I'm asking you to stay out of it, and let me do the dirty work. I promise, I'll get him home safely."

Commendable, yes, but not what my ex-boyfriend wanted. "He cast a spell to make me forget how I feel for him."

"A spell? I wasn't aware of that. Did it work?"

I shook my head. "I guess my feelings for him broke through."

His eyes softened. "That must be a powerful love."

A smile tugged at the corners of my mouth. "I can't argue that."

"Listen." He crouched down to pet Cooper who had plopped onto the back of the couch to keep tabs on the strange, large, monster of a man, without kinking his neck. "We both know that no matter what I say, you're going to look for him, and you're going to hunt down the mountain man. At least let me help. Trust me, you can't do it alone, and I can protect you that way."

"And keep your promise to Gabe."

"Yes."

"I have Remmington and a bunch of other magicals who will help me. I don't even know what you are, and I don't know if I can trust you."

"Understood. I'm a high-level warlock. Modern human terminology might call someone similar a high priest, but that is a basic definition. I am not technically a priest in the Wiccan sense, but I am one with powers above any you can even begin to imagine."

His alien-like tone had normalized, as if I'd been talking to any old magical, not one who ranked himself at the level of a high priest.

I pursed my lips. "If that's true, why can't you just flick your wrist or something and bring Gabe back?"

"It's complicated, and you know magic doesn't work that way."

He was right, but that didn't mean I liked it. "How can I trust you?"

"I understand trust is earned, and I'm asking you to give me the opportunity to earn it."

I dragged my top teeth over my bottom lip. He was right. I wouldn't stop until I found Gabe and caught the mountain man, but I had no clue where to start or how to go about it. I needed help, and someone at his level could provide that. Plus, he had access to information I didn't, and I might need that information. Trusting him was the problem. But again, he was right. Trust was earned. I wanted to find Gabe, but was allowing someone I'd just met to earn my trust the only way to do that? "I have no leads, no suspects, not even any guesses as to what might be going on. How are we supposed to start?" I shook my head. I wasn't sure working with a stranger was a good idea, but then again, my options were limited.

Cooper spoke as if he'd read my mind. "What do you have to lose?"

"My life. Your life. Gabe's life?"

"All things you stand to lose if you go at it on your own as well," Cooper said.

I hated it when my familiar cat was right. "Fine," I said to Kaeden. "We'll give this a shot. You have a week, and then you're out."

He smirked. "I won't need that long."

"Right," I said with a sly smile. "We'll see about that."

"Abby, it's important that you remember this phrase. *The vision is mine to see.* Can you do that?"

"Uh, sure. I guess. Why?"

"You'll know when it's necessary."

Kaedan left after insisting I sleep, claiming both Cooper and I would need our strength to work with him. He promised to meet us later that following morning at the Enchanted.

4

To my surprise, I slept like a baby, waking up at close to eight o'clock, and only because Cooper sat on my chest and breathed into my face, repeating, *Abby, the tuna is calling*, like a broken record.

The vision is mine to see echoed in my mind. What did that even mean? Was it important to finding Gabe? Could it lead us to him or the mountain man?

We made it to the café in thirty minutes. Stella was already sitting at our regular table watching Mr. Hastings and Bessie giggle and smile near the fireplace.

"I can't even with the cuteness," she said. "It's like their budding relationship brought out some new old man who no longer cranks his foul attitude into high gear on the regular."

"He's super nice now. It's weird."

"Right?" She sipped her coffee. "It's very weird."

"Most things in the world are." I walked behind the counter and poured myself a cup of coffee. Bessie hadn't even noticed me. It was definitely weird.

"And speaking of weird," Stella said as I sat down. "Remmington came in looking for you already. Why are you so late?"

I grinned at Cooper who stared at Bessie and Waylon Hastings with a confused look on his face. Mr. Charming sat on his perch repeating, *Bessie and Waylon sitting in a tree*, over and over. "I stayed up late and slept in. When was he here?"

"About fifteen minutes ago. Bessie offered him one of her new cinnamon lattes for free, but he declined. It was weird. I don't think anyone's ever said no to one of Bessie's specialty coffees, but he claims cinnamon bothers his stomach." She tilted her head. "Everything okay? Did something happen between you and the hottie?"

"Remmington and I are only casually dating," I said, though that wasn't entirely true. We hadn't defined it as anything specific, and in dating terms, casually dating was a definition. "There's not much that could happen."

"Uh, wrong on so many levels." She sipped her coffee again. "That's when things do happen. It's when relationships are defined. Did you two have an argument?"

"No."

"So, everything's okay?"

"Yes, it's fine. I just stayed up late working on my manuscript. It happens."

"Why didn't you just say that then?"

"I would have had I known I'd get the third degree."

She blinked. "Whoa. Crabby much?"

"Much, apparently. Sorry, I didn't realize until I heard how I sounded just now."

"Gabe again?"

"I'm not talking about Gabe."

She nodded once. "Definitely Gabe again."

A slim man with short, dark hair walked into the café.

He was dressed in dark jeans, a black sweater, and a pair of cowboy boots. A thick bluish gray pit bull walked close beside him.

Cooper raced back to my lap. "Uh, that thing wants to eat me."

Stella and I stared as the man directed the dog to a table near the wall and commanded him to sit. The dog sat.

"Is he going to leash that monster?" Stella asked.

"Look at the drool dripping from his mouth," Cooper said. "That's him preparing to gulp me down as his morning snack."

"The dog is not a monster, and he's not going to eat Cooper," I said.

Stella laughed. "I didn't say that."

"No, but I'm sure Cooper's thinking it."

"How can you be sure he won't?" Cooper asked. "Look at that jaw. It's bigger than me."

"The dog hasn't even glanced at us. He's watching his person," I said.

Mr. Charming hopped off his perch and onto the counter as Bessie walked over. "Coffee. Where's my coffee?"

The man's mouth twitched. Bessie rushed behind the counter. "Don't mind him. He's stuck on repeat."

He laughed. "I bet that's entertaining."

"You have no idea." She turned her head toward the menu on the wall behind her. "What can I get you?"

"Just a black coffee, please."

"Sure thing. I'll bring it right over." She grinned at the dog. "That's a gorgeous, well-trained dog."

"Thank you. Brutus has been with me a long time. He's only tough when I tell him to be."

"Is that often?" she asked.

"Not lately."

"Go on and have a seat."

"Yes, ma'am."

Stella gathered her things. "Well, I'm out of here."

"Really? I just got here."

She angled her head toward the dog. "It's the drool." She shuddered. "I can't with that."

"I can relate to that," Cooper said.

"I understand," I said. "I'll call you later."

"I know." She hiked her bag over her shoulder and nearly jogged to the door.

After Bessie brought the man his coffee and went back to Waylon, the man smiled at me. Something about him felt familiar, but I couldn't quite put my finger on it.

Cooper's little brick of a body stiffened as he stood and walked over. The dog by his side. "He's coming for me! That slobbering meat grinder is headed straight for me!" He jumped onto my lap and burrowed his head under his front legs.

Wasn't my familiar supposed to protect me? "Wow, such a brave kitty. Thanks for watching over me."

"All bets are off when I'm in danger of being some mutt's breakfast."

"Nice. Real nice."

Cooper leaned his head less than an inch closer to them and sniffed him. He jerked his head back. I appreciated my familiar's desire to protect me, but at times, it was annoying. That was one of those times. The dog wasn't going to attack. He even appeared to be smiling.

The man smiled. Had he understood Cooper? That familiar thing nudged the back of my mind. I knew him. I just couldn't figure out how. "Good morning, Abby. You ready to get started?"

I blinked. "I'm sorry. Do I know you?"

The corners of his mouth curved up, then he pulled out a chair and sat next to me. Cooper hissed at him and the dog, but the dog just sat on the ground next to his person, still not at all interested in either of us. The man removed a small, folded paper from his pocket and slid it across the table. I glanced at the paper and then up at him. He nodded once, so I opened the paper. It read, *Say the phrase.*

I refolded the paper and looked back at the man. "The vision is mine to see?" I watched as the words sailed through the air. Their energy grew bigger and swirled around the man. As it encased him, his appearance changed into Kaedan. He grinned, placed two fingers on the paper I'd set back on the table, slid it back to him, then instantly returned to the stranger in front of me.

"Undercover work often requires alternate appearances. It may or may not happen again," he said. "But if it does, you'll need to use the phrase when you think it might be me. If you're wrong, you won't see me. You'll see the person or magical they truly are."

My eyes widened. "Uh, okay." And I thought it was some secret to finding Gabe. What a downer that was.

"What about the dog?" Cooper asked. "Is he really a mouse disguised as a vicious cat killer, because a mouse, I can handle. I don't like them, but I can handle them."

"Can you understand my cat?"

He shook his head. "I just assumed you were talking to him."

"I was. Is the dog a real dog?" My voice came out sounding annoyed, but I wasn't.

"The dog is many things," Kaedan said. "But always, he is loyal to me. He won't act unless I tell him to."

"Understood," I said.

"Miss Odell," he said in a more formal tone than I'd

expected. "I am Bryant Cumberland, and this is my dog Brutus." He winked.

"Nice to meet you, Mr. Cumberland."

"Please, call me Bryant."

"Okay."

"You might be wondering why I'm here, so I'll explain." He winked once more. "I am here to investigate Gabe Reynolds. I understand you have information regarding his work with the MBI?"

My eyes shifted toward Bessie and Waylon. Waylon raised a brow. Since they watched me closely, I decided playing along was important. I hated deceiving Bessie, but I'd tell her the truth once Gabe was safe and the mountain man was banished to wherever the higher-ups chose. I leaned back in my chair and crossed my arms over my chest. "If I did, why would I share it with you?"

"It would be in your best interests, Miss Odell."

Mr. Charming flew over and perched on the bookcase behind us. I flipped around and gave him a quick glance. He'd puffed out his feathers and was staring at Brutus with such intensity, I thought he might attack. "It's okay, Mr. Charming. I've got this." I snuck a peek at Cooper who'd sat glued to my lap. "At least someone's trying to protect me."

"Hey," he said. "I thought we were safe."

"Good point," I said. I grinned at Kaedan. I'd have to get used to that. "What kind of information are you looking for?"

"I've set up a small mobile office inside a van outside. I'd like to discuss it there."

I raised an eyebrow. "Uh…"

Bessie rushed over. "Sir, may I see some identification, please?"

A smile washed over my face. "Bessie, I love you, but I've

got this." I turned back toward Kaedan. "Yes, identification would be great."

He smiled as he removed his wallet from his pocket and then showed an identification card with his photo to me and then to Bessie. "You may check with the MBI," he said. He grinned at Bessie. "They will verify my assignment."

Her eyes shifted to me. I nodded once. I thought he'd be verified, but I wanted to make her comfortable. She walked into the kitchen. Mr. Charming and Waylon each followed.

"She will get confirmation, right?" I asked.

"Yes."

A few minutes later, Bessie returned. "Thank you, Mr. Cumberland. I appreciate your department finally showing interest in helping my Abby with her situation." She smiled, nodded to me, and then hiked back to the kitchen.

I leaned over the table and whispered, "Who did she talk to at the MBI?"

"Me." He stood. "Let's go."

I grabbed Cooper, and we left.

He'd parked a large, black, windowless van at the corner of the road. Inside, the van setup boasted the most advanced human technology I'd ever seen. Granted, I hadn't seen much more than what was in movies, but the flashing lights, the rhythmic beeps, and engine sounds bringing it to life were telltale signs to the equipment's importance. "Is this stuff why we're in the van?"

Cooper jumped on a large keyboard. Kaedan picked him up and set him on the floor.

"The protection surrounding this is stronger than anything we could create together. As it stands now, no magicals or humans know we're here. Even members of the MBI. The van and everything in it is invisible to all."

"That's crazy. Powerful, but crazy. How is it possible?"

"My powers are limitless." His energy changed back to Kaedan. "And frankly, I prefer being my true self instead of in disguise."

"Makes sense." He offered me a seat in the small chair while he sat in the larger one. "So, what happens now?"

"I've already started the search." He pointed to a TV-style screen. "This is the topography of the area where Gabe was last seen. These dots," he pointed to a red one and a green one, are humans and magicals. The humans are in the red, and the magicals are in the green."

"How do you know if one of those is Gabe?"

He pointed to one of the green moving dots. "A number pops up when I touch the screen." He tapped the screen with his finger, and the number six hundred and two appeared. "That is Agent Hermandos." He stretched to his right and handed me a three-ring binder filled with hundreds of pieces of paper. "This is the list of all MBI staff. Each one is assigned a number. Gabe's number is twenty-two."

I checked the numbers, and he was right. "Are these in any kind of order?"

"Yes. Number one is the first MBI agent, and the most recent is upwards of seven thousand."

"How long has the MBI been around?"

"Since the 1700s."

My jaw dropped. I knew Gabe had been around a while, and in human years, he was a bit older than me, but not as old as a warlock who was a magical in the 1700s. How was I supposed to wrap my head around that?

The corner of Kaedan's mouth twitched. "How old did you think he was?"

"A lot younger than that."

"It must be hard transitioning from believing you're a

human and living a human life to discovering you're a witch and living a magical life."

"You have no idea."

"We've been watching for Gabe for months now, but with no luck. He went rogue shortly after starting the assignment, and several magicals have been assigned the task of finding him, including me."

My breath caught in my throat. "Rogue? You didn't tell me that. I've seen him since he left, and he hasn't mentioned that either. Why would he go rogue?"

"I have a theory, but I thought you'd know something."

"I have no idea. I don't understand what's going on. What was his assignment in the first place?"

He handed me a file folder. "It's all in there. He was assigned the task of locating an evil-infected warlock by the name of Dexius Kredum. There's a picture of him inside the file."

I opened the folder and stared right into the mountain man's face. I lifted my eyes to Kaedan's. "This is the mountain man." I held up the picture and shook it. My heart raced, causing my blood to sprint through my veins. "This is the man coming to me in my dreams and telling me Gabe's not coming home. This is the man Gabe claims to be protecting me from. He's the man after Gabe."

"Yes."

"Yes? That's all you have to say? Yes? I already knew about the mountain man. I already knew Gabe was on the hunt for him. What is it you're not telling me?"

He exhaled. "Dexius Kredum is Gabe's brother."

5

Unbelievable. After lifting my jaw up from the van's floor, I asked, "Are you serious?"

"The MBI believes Gabe's teamed up with his brother, but I don't believe it. I think he's pretending, so he can bring his brother in."

"And that's what you mean by 'going rogue'?"

"It's the only explanation I can come up with. My other option is to believe the MBI is right, and Gabe's gone dark."

I shook my head. "Gabe isn't the type of magical to go against what he's believed for, well, I guess hundreds of years now." Cooper hopped on my lap. I petted him without even thinking about it. "He would never go rogue. Not unless it was an act, and then his intentions would be good, so it wouldn't be real anyway."

"I'm not disagreeing with you, but the MBI sees this differently. We have to find Gabe before they do, so we can warn him that he's running out of time."

"Running out of time for what?"

He stared at the screen on the large computer. "His brother is evil. This is all about his brother."

I rattled off a list of questions. "What did his brother do? Why do they want him? Why is he evil?" My hands shook, and something heavy settled in the pit of my stomach.

"He's murdered three very important members of our elite team, a team directly in contact with the powers that be."

I tipped my head back and closed my eyes, letting that all sink in. When I finally had come to terms with it as much as I could, I asked, "How are we going to find him?"

He pointed to the monstrosity of equipment stuffed into the van. "This will help."

"Great. I can type and print, and printing is questionable."

"I'll show you what to do."

Seven hours later, we'd tracked Gabe about two months before along a path through Georgia, Tennessee, and then back to Georgia, where we lost him south of Holiday Hills. He'd gone completely dark.

"How is that possible?" I asked. "Shouldn't the MBI have something to keep tabs on their agents?"

"They do," he said. "But Gabe's a powerful warlock, and he knows how to block the systems."

"Like you did with this van?"

"Yes."

"Do you think he's changing his appearance like you as well?"

"Yes."

I sighed. "Then how are we supposed to find him?"

"Faith, Abby. Faith."

Faith didn't get us very far.

∼

Cooper and I curled up on the couch together, me under a sherpa throw and him on top of my hip. I tried not to think about Gabe's connection to the mountain man, but it kept knocking on my brain. Why hadn't he told me about him? Why hadn't he even mentioned Dexius Kredum in passing? The more I thought about it, the more I realized he hadn't talked about his family much at all. Was it because of Dexius or was he hiding something else?

"You're thinking too much," Cooper said.

"I am not."

"Ab, I can feel your blood rushing through your veins. Your heart rate's soaring." He stared at the ceiling. "Yup, one hundred fifty-five beats per minute. That's anaerobic. You need to relax."

I shifted my hips, and he slid between me and the back of the couch. Poor Cooper was so small he got stuck in between the cushions and the couch back.

"Uh, little help here, please?"

I lifted him out of the tight space. "My bad." I set him on the back of the couch. I didn't want him analyzing my health any further.

"Take a deep breath. Come on. In ... and hold it. Then slowly blow it out." He followed his directions as he spoke.

My anxiety lessened after three rounds of kitty yoga breathing. "If Gabe's brother was evil, he would have told me."

"Except he didn't tell you he even had a brother. Isn't that kind of the same thing?"

"Yes. No. Maybe? I thought we shared everything."

"Maybe he didn't tell you because he's ashamed."

I climbed off the couch and walked into the kitchen saying, "I really hate when you read my mind. But," I exaggerated my tone. "Something doesn't feel right about any of this. I can't quite put my finger on it, but it doesn't feel right."

"I knew you thought that as well."

"Stop reading my mind."

"It's my job to protect you, and we're connected." He hopped off the back of the couch and followed me.

"But that's weird."

"Ain't that the truth? Some of the things going on in your head? Yeah, I'd rather not know."

"Like what?" I poured myself a cup of milk and heated it in the microwave. Warm milk relaxed me and reminded me of my childhood. How I wished my mother was still alive. I could have used her advice.

"I'm not saying." He shook his tiny head. "I can't even think about some of that girly stuff."

A rush of heat filled my cheeks. "Yikes. I think I know what you're talking about."

He turned and walked out of the kitchen. I followed behind. "I bet you—"

We froze.

6

"Abby, it's not... I'm not..."

The mountain man collapsed into a heap on my floor. "Is he dead?" Cooper asked. "I don't know," I said. I rushed the few feet to him. Blood seeped from the side of his chest. "I think he's been shot!" I dropped to my knees and checked for a pulse on the side of his neck. I had to move his ratty, dirty hair to find the right spot. He had a fire flame tattooed on his artery. It was beating, but barely. I held out my hand and said, "Cell phone!" It appeared in my hand. I dialed magical 911 and asked for an ambulance.

Time passed in slow motion during the three minutes it took for the ambulance to arrive. I checked his pulse but couldn't feel anything, so I administered CPR while casting spell after spell to heal Dexius or at least keep him alive. Keeping him there could bring back Gabe or lead us to him. The paramedics knocked just as I called for a defibrillator. I blinked the door open, and two women dropped down and took over CPR, counting and breathing in rhythm.

"We've got a pulse," one of the paramedics said.

I leaned back against the side of the couch, question upon question racing through my brain. Why had he come? What happened to him? Where was Gabe?

"Miss, are you okay?" A young paramedic with short black hair and full red lips stuck his face close to mine. "Miss?"

I shook my head. "Yes, I'm fine. Just a little freaked out." He asked me what happened, and I told him.

Remmington stormed in, pushed the paramedic to the side, and grabbed me. "Abby?" He crouched down next to me. "Are you okay? What happened?"

"I'm fine. The ... it's the mountain man," I whispered. "He's been shot."

The paramedics stopped working on Dexius. "I'm not sure he's going to make it," one of them said.

My body went numb.

~

Since Remmington was the chief, he'd made sure only magicals handled Dexius's case, so I wouldn't have to answer any questions I'd struggle to answer, and it wouldn't be recorded on anything humans used. He felt obligated to go back to the department after his officer finished my interview, and I was relieved because I had something important to do.

"Kaedan? Kaedan, can you hear me?" I stood on the floor next to where Dexius Kredum had lain bleeding. A patch of blood stained my throw rug. I flicked my hand, and it disappeared.

Kaedan appeared. He looked as he had the first time I had met him. "What's going on? Are you okay?"

"It's Dexius Kredum. He's been shot. The magicals have

taken him. That means Gabe can come home. We need to find a way to let him know."

His eyes widened. "How do you know?"

"Because he appeared right there and died. Someone shot him in the chest. He died, Kaedan, but the paramedics revived him. Gabe needs to know."

He stepped closer. "How can you be sure it was him?"

"That man has invaded my dreams for months. I know him in the pit of my soul. What I don't understand is why he came here after being shot. Did he think I'd help him? After all he did to me? To Gabe?"

"But you did help him."

I dropped onto my couch and pulled my knees to my chest. "I couldn't help it. It was just an automatic reaction." I stared up at Kaeden. "What's going on?" Cooper sat on the couch back above me.

Kaedan sat next to me. "We need to know if it's really him. Where did they take him?"

"I don't know. I can ask Remmington."

"No, don't. It's okay. I'll find him."

"How will you know it's him?"

"Because Dexius Kredum has a fire flame tattooed on his neck."

"Then it's him." I sighed. "I checked his pulse and saw it."

He leaned his head back and nodded. "That doesn't mean it's him. It could be a magical that's morphed into him. We'll need to make sure."

"How do you suppose we do that?"

"Simple magic."

"Fine, but if it's him, then the MBI can cancel the mission, and Gabe can come home, right?"

He shook his head. "He can't come out of hiding. Not yet.

Attempted murder is just as bad as murder, whether it's an evil warlock or an innocent bystander. The MBI will seek justice, and that could mean banishment or prison for Gabe."

I rubbed my temples. "Wait a minute, are you saying Gabe tried to murder his brother?"

"I'm saying the MBI might believe that."

"But he'd do it out of self-defense. He wouldn't shoot his brother just because. That's not Gabe."

"You said the victim was shot in the chest, right?"

"Yes."

"That's Gabe's signature shot."

"Meaning when Gabe kills people, that's what he does? Shoots them in the chest? Does Gabe kill or try to kill a lot of people?"

"Gabe had a very important job with the bureau, and witchcraft aside, he is a very powerful and dangerous warlock."

I needed to move. My blood soared through my veins, and a pit of anxiety hardened my stomach. If I sat there any longer, I would explode. I stood and paced the floor in front of my coffee table. "I've never thought of Gabe that way. I mean, yes, he was the chief of police, and yes, I saw him do things because of his positions with the police and the bureau, but I just thought of him as a kindhearted warlock. Why would they punish him for attempting to kill his brother when they sent him out looking for him in the first place? Like I said, if it was Gabe who shot him, it had to be self-defense."

"They wanted him to bring Dexius in alive and without injury. Gabe understood the assignment. If he shot him, then something went wrong. And if that's the case, then he'll go too dark for us to locate him. The only way we'll see him again is if he can prove what happened and prove his innocence."

"No." I shook my head. "We can find him. I'm a powerful witch, and you're a warlock on steroids. If anybody can find Gabe, it's us."

Cooper meowed. "A warlock on steroids. That's a good one."

"Abby, you can't just flick your wrist and make things happen."

Cooper said, "Um, yes, she can."

"I don't care," I said. "We have to at least try." I waved my hand. "And if you don't want to help, I'll just do it myself."

7

The next morning, without a hint of sleep, I rolled out of bed disillusioned and disheveled. I stared at my reflection in the mirror wondering how the bright-faced witch I'd been could be that pale one with dark circles and bags bigger than my suitcase hanging below her eyes. Exhausted wasn't a strong enough word to explain how I felt. I splashed cold water on my face, dropped a few squirts of eye drops into my eyes, and then brushed my teeth. I combed the knots out of my hair, realized it needed a washing, and flicked my wrist to create the illusion of good hygiene and styled hair. What was the saying? Fake it till you make it? That was what I had done. At least the first part.

Cooper raced down the stairs to the Enchanted, burst through the door and darted straight to the kitchen. I said hello to the regulars, then extended my arm for Mr. Charming to hop on. "Hello, Mr. Charming. You look lovely today."

"Hello. Hello. Mr. Charming is lovely. Mr. Charming is lovely."

Stella waved from our table. "Hurry, but leave the bird over there."

I kept Mr. Charming with me. "Stella loves Mr. Charming."

He hollered for her in a deep, blues singer-sounding voice. "Stella! Stella!"

I sauntered to the table, bird on my arm and a pretend smile plastered onto my face, faking it until I made it, which I hoped would be soon. I set my purse on the table. "He loves you."

She cringed. Stella and Mr. Charming had a unique relationship. He freaked Stella out, and his feelings for her changed by the minute. He liked to play with her. Mr. Charming might have seemed like just a parrot, but he was a very smart and very territorial familiar. I never understood the dynamics of their relationship, but it hadn't changed in years.

Mr. Charming climbed down my arm and perched on a chair back. "Sad. Abby is sad."

I pursed my lips. "What? I'm not sad. Why would you say that?"

"Gabe is gone. Gabe is gone."

"Okay bird, that's enough," Stella said. "She knows he's gone. Don't rub it in."

Wow. She'd stood up to the bird. That was unexpected. "Thank you."

Mr. Charming said, "Kisses? Hmm. Want kisses?"

I gave him a smooch on the beak. "Good kisses."

"Good kisses," he said. He flew to the kitchen door, landed on the ground, and pushed it open with his beak.

"Okay," Stella said. She examined me closely, her eyes sticking on almost every detail of my being. "What's wrong? It's Gabe again, isn't it? Abby, I love you, but you've got to let this go. Gabe is gone, and you don't know when or if he's ever coming back."

"He's coming back, Stella. I know it."

"Fine, he's coming back. Does that mean you have to spend every second of your life while he's gone sinking into some bottomless pit of angst and trepidation because you haven't heard from him? He's working a very important mission. I doubt he can tell the criminals, *Hey, hold on. I need to call my girlfriend and let her know I'm good*."

"You're wrong." I cringed. "I'm not doing any of that," I lied. "Don't listen to Mr. Charming. He just repeats things he's heard before. You know that."

She raised an eyebrow. "Right."

"I'm fine," I said with deliberateness. "I promise."

She crossed her arms over her chest. "Remmington came in a little while ago. He was looking for you. Said to let you know it's all been handled. Care to tell me what he's talking about?"

"I just asked him to get some information for my book, that's it. Nothing serious." I hated lying to Stella, but sometimes it was my only choice.

"Where's your laptop bag?"

"Oh, I'm not working today. I've got an appointment in Cumming."

Her eyes widened. "Really? What's up?"

"What's with the interrogation? Can't a girl just have an appointment?"

"Abby Odell, I am your best friend." She waved her hand and made a circle around my face. "You can dress it up however you want, but I know when something's going on."

She was good. Really good.

"What else could it be?"

She exhaled. "Okay, let me try and say it in a way you

might understand. Gabe dumped you. He's gone, and who knows if he's coming back? Remmington is here. He adores you. He'd do anything for you, and you like him. Why can't you let go of Gabe?"

Love was a powerful emotion. So powerful, it was the only emotion to break through spells. Like the one Gabe had cast on me shortly after he'd left. No matter what he thought best, my love for him had overpowered and voided his spell on me. He should have known that would happen. I checked my watch. "I need a coffee, and then I have to go."

She rolled her eyes. "Fine, but we're going to talk about this again."

I stood and headed toward the kitchen saying, "I have no doubt about that."

8

Kaedan was missing in action, so I decided to do what I could. I needed to know more about Gabe. In a short time, I'd learned things I never thought possible, and there had to be more. There had to be something that could lead me to the information and answers I needed, and the best place to learn that was his house.

"Where are we going?" Cooper asked. I'd put him in the car and tossed my purse on the passenger's side floor.

"To Gabe's house."

"Why?"

"Because everything about Gabe is there, and it's the best place to look for information about his investigation." Mostly, it was the only idea I had, but the rest was also true.

Gabe's place was on the border of Holiday Hills and the next town. Really the town was a county, but they'd called it a town because there was only one town in that entire county. Bramblett County was full of nice people, but no magicals lived there. I didn't travel into their space often because I never had a reason.

On a whim, Gabe had moved shortly before leaving for his mission. He'd said he wanted a change of scenery, but I wondered if it had something to do with his brother.

The drive was a straight shot down a long two-way road followed by one left turn. His house was the second on the right. I parked in the driveway and eyed his place. Was I making the right decision, or would it make things worse? We'd shared memories there. I knew where his dishes went, how his laundry always landed in front of his basket instead of in it. I'd even bought him a bigger basket, but he'd still thrown his clothing beside it. I knew the cracks in the ceiling, and most importantly where he hid his spare key. I had to go in. Memories or not, I needed to see if I could find anything that would lead me to Gabe. If the key wasn't there, I'd just use magic to get inside.

The key was still where he'd hidden it months ago. I unlocked the door and took a deep breath before going in.

Cooper waited for me before he charged in. "Well," he said. He wandered around the family room. "Looks like it did the last time we were here." He rushed to the kitchen and climbed on the counter next to the pantry.

The house was one of those open floor plans where everything was visible from the front and back doors. I wasn't sure it was what I'd have chosen, but Gabe loved it.

Cooper reached over to the pantry door handle and pushed down on it with his paw. When it unlatched, he stuck his paw between it and the frame and nudged the door open. He climbed down the counter and opened the door further with a shove from his side. "He's got salmon, but no tuna. Third shelf up on the right." He stepped out and looked up at me with his big brown eyes. "Do me a solid, will ya?"

"Do you a solid?"

"Yeah, you know, a solid. Like a favor. Do me a favor."

"We're not here to eat. We're here to look for hints to find Gabe."

"I know, but you can't expect me to do that on an empty stomach."

"You literally just ate at the Enchanted. Not even an hour ago."

"I'm small, and I metabolize food fast. Why do you think cats sleep so much?"

"Because they're bored and lazy."

"Well, yeah, but it's mostly because we digest and use our food fast, and you people only feed us one or two times a day, so we're basically starving, which makes us exhausted and bored and lazy."

I wasn't about to debate that. I had more important things to do. "Fine. But don't leave a mess." I grabbed the can of salmon and opened it, then put it on the floor.

"I never leave a mess."

"Uh, yes, you do. You leave little bits of tuna everywhere you eat. Bessie's counter. My floor. Stella's carpeted bedroom where you've also thrown up."

"Everyone knows you don't feed cats on carpet. It's a magnet for cat yack."

"I'm going to look around," I said and headed to Gabe's office.

I stood just outside his office door and stared at the room. Except for his laundry, he was a neat freak, and everything had a place. I asked him about it, and he'd told me the laundry didn't matter, because he did it every few days. I wasn't a neat freak by any means, but I'd always put my laundry in a basket. Sometimes, I'd even leave the clean stuff in one for weeks.

He'd bought new bookcases for his new place, and we'd

spent an evening going through his things, then organizing what he'd kept, and putting it away. I stepped into the room and over to the bookcases, dragging my fingers along the middle shelf on each one. When I touched the last one, a shock of electricity soared through my body. I jumped back and hit the front of his desk. I closed my eyes and shook my head, and when I opened them, I saw Gabe and I organizing the shelves.

"Here," he said. He handed me an empty box. "Use this for garbage."

I tossed old files he'd approved as garbage into the box.

He glanced inside and said, "Oh, wait." He removed a file. "I need this one."

"Yeah?" I winked. "Is it all the details of your past girlfriends?"

He smiled, put the file on his legs, and kissed me. "No one in my past or future will ever be as important as you."

"Now, I'm intrigued," I said. He picked up the file and waved it at me. I tried to grab it, but he jerked it away. I stuck out my bottom lip and pouted. "That's mean."

"Some things are meant to be kept secret."

"Until they're not," I said.

"And when it's that time, you'll know. I promise." He pointed to the closet. The door opened, and a large safe appeared. He walked over and unlocked the safe with a passcode, placed the file inside, then closed the steel door.

The vision disappeared. "That's right! The safe." Gabe had intentionally done that, so I'd know where it was. He'd left something for me. Something that he thought I'd need. I raced to the closet and swung open the door only to find an empty plastic storage bin and no safe. I stared at the storage bin. What would Gabe do? Would he have hidden the safe from view or disguised it as something basic? I wasn't sure, but I'd figure it out. I pointed to the bin and swirled my finger. "Plastic bin on the floor, show me what you were before."

The safe appeared. I nearly cried. Cooper walked in. "I was going to say to look in the safe, but I got distracted."

"I need the passcode."

He climbed onto the desk. "Don't look at me. Gabe and I didn't have a sharing kind a relationship."

I walked over to the desk and leaned my bottom against it. Staring at the safe, I tried hard to go back to that moment and watch Gabe's fingers type in the code, but I couldn't get there. "It's got to be something easy for him to remember."

"His birthday? Your birthday? His mom's birthday? His phone number? His mom's phone number? The phone number he had as a kid? His parents' anniversary? The date you two started dating?" He leaned against me. "That's all I've got."

I chewed on my fingernail. "I don't know any of the phone numbers, and I only know his birthday. He never talked about his family, remember?" I walked back to the safe. "I'll try his birthday first, and if it's not that, we'll try something else." I typed in what I knew to be Gabe's celebrated human birthday. I had no idea when he was born other than it was a lot longer ago then I'd thought. The safe lock didn't click open. "It's not his birthday."

"The day you started dating?"

"Why would he use that?" I asked.

"I don't know. It's just a suggestion." He scratched his side. "Don't shoot the suggestion maker."

"I'll try it." I tapped in the numbers, but nothing happened. I chewed the same nail and thought about what it could have been. I tried his street address, my street address, the Enchanted's street address, but nothing worked. "I don't know what to do. It could be anything. The combination of numbers is endless."

"But not impossible to run through," Cooper said. "Just cast a spell to figure out the code."

There were rules to being a witch. I'd learned to follow most of them, but Cooper's suggestion pushed the limit. Was I searching for Gabe for my benefit or his? Truthfully, a little of both. Personal gain was a big no-no for magicals, but I'd done it before—and so had Bessie—and hadn't been punished, so maybe it wasn't as big of an issue as the powers that be wanted us to believe? I figured doing it again with a mix of intentions couldn't get me in too much trouble, and if it did, I'd deal with it.

"Passcode, passcode, shine your light? Run the numbers until they're right."

Cooper meowed. "Really? That's lame, Ab."

"You know I don't cast spells well under pressure."

The lock lit up as the spell worked through the numbers. I held my breath and waited. When it clicked open, I yelped with joy. I stared at it, afraid to move. Afraid to see what Gabe kept locked up and hidden from both worlds.

"Well? You going to get it, or should I?" Cooper asked.

"I'm working on it." I stepped closer. Was it wrong, searching through Gabe's private files? Was I being selfish? Why hadn't I thought that before? Would he do it if the tables were turned? Yes. Yes, he would do it. And he'd know I would do it as well. I gasped. He'd know I'd do it as well! I have to be right. He showed me the safe in case I needed something, and I do. "There's something in there, Coop. Something important."

"Then what're you waiting for?"

"Right." I nodded. "Right!" I dove to the safe and

searched through the files, hoping I'd know what I needed when I saw it.

And I did. "Here," I said waving the file. "This is it!" I moved to the side, sat on the floor, and opened the file on my lap. I stared at the thirty-page, double-sided, typed document. I read the title out loud. "Dexius K. Kredum. It's about his brother."

"His brother has middle initials?"

"Most everyone does, and is that really your first thought?"

"No, my first thought was, hurry and read it. I need to use the facilities."

"Just go," I said.

"Gabe doesn't have a litter box."

"Use the toilet. You know how to do it."

"I hate doing that. I'm afraid I'll lose my balance, and no one wants to fall into a toilet, especially a cat who hates water."

I narrowed my eyes at him. "Cooper!"

"Fine," he said and left the room.

I read the contents of the document quickly. The details frightened me. Dexius K. Kredum was evil. The information claimed he'd been born that way, and pretended to be good, but as time passed, he'd become worse. At one point, the MBI had arrested and imprisoned him, but he'd somehow escaped. The powers that be had attempted to bind his powers, but they'd been unsuccessful, which meant he'd made a deal with the devil, literally.

I couldn't understand why Gabe had been assigned to hunt down his own brother. Someone that evil? Why would the MBI do that? They'd have to know how complicated that would be, even for a magical. Yet, they'd assigned him with the job.

Or had he asked for it?

Cooper returned. "What's it say?"

"It's a history of the crimes Dexius Kredum has committed. All the details, the locations, the victims. Everything. Just nothing to lead me to Gabe."

"What about the locations of his crimes? Could you start with those? They might lead us in the right direction if anything."

I exhaled. "They're everywhere. He even pretended to be a cop once. I don't think the location's it. Gabe said I'd know when it was time."

"What're you talking about?"

"I saw back in time when we organized the office. I think he showed me this on purpose. But it's not this file. It's got to be something else." I removed the rest of the files and searched through them. When I saw the one with my name written on it, I knew I'd found what I needed. "This!"

Cooper sat beside me as I opened the file. Inside was an envelope, the kind businesses used to send documents they didn't want folded. "It feels empty?"

"That's good. The less in there, the easier this should be, right?"

"Or the opposite," I said.

"Change your mindset, Ab."

I took a deep breath and opened it carefully, worried I might destroy something I'd need. Inside was one piece of paper. I read it out loud.

My Dearest Abby,

You remembered the day we organized my office. I'm so glad. I hoped you'd get the message back then. I wasn't sure you'd need it, but if you're reading this, you did.

By now, I'm assuming you know about Dexius. There much too much to the story to go into a letter, but know that things aren't always as they seem. I'm sorry I didn't tell you, but I wanted to keep you safe. I've asked the MBI to let me search for him. I've gone dark, and you won't see me until I finish my mission. Do you understand what that means? I know I've always said I'd come if you called, no matter where I am, but if you call for me, know it isn't me who came. It is someone very, very dangerous. Do not let the imposter fool you, and do not try to capture him. He is too powerful. I will finish my mission, and when I do, I promise, I will return to you.

All my love,

Gabe

I flipped the paper over. The back was dated earlier that morning. "He's been here. He was here this morning!" I shoved the note in Cooper's face. "Look!"

"Well, don't just show me it, read the dang thing!"

"Oh, right." I read it out loud.

Dearest Abby,

It wasn't me who cast the spell over you, and it wasn't Dexius in your apartment. I know you're looking for me. Please stop. It is far more dangerous than you think. Please, watch who you trust. I am safe, and I am closer than you think, but I am close to completing my mission, and I won't stop until it's done. I will return home, and you'll know it's me. That's all I can say without putting you in danger. Please, let this go.

Abby, I understand about Remmington. Your choices are yours. Just be careful.

All my love,

Gabe

Cooper meowed. "Okay, let's think about this for a minute. If Gabe wrote that letter and brought it here, why wouldn't he just come to you with his warnings?"

"Maybe he knew I'd be upset if he didn't stay?"

He sat and stared up at me.

"He could have written the letter and sent it here magically," I said.

"Or maybe he didn't write it at all?"

I shook my head. "No. It's from him."

"How do you know?"

"I just do," I said. "I just do."

9

I held the letter in my hand and stared at Cooper. "What do you think it means?"

"In a nutshell? To stay out of it."

I glared at him. "That's not helpful."

"Maybe not," he said. He stretched on the floor. "But it's the truth. If it was him that wrote it, he made it clear. Let him do his job, and he'll be back."

"But what if he needs help?"

"If he does, he'll find you or what's his face." He scratched his ear. "Kaedan."

"He's kept his eye on me this whole time. He knows I've been seeing Remmington." I ran my hand through my hair. "I feel awful. I thought that was what he wanted, for me to move on, but it wasn't him. He didn't cast the spell on me. Now what am I supposed to do?"

"He said he understood about Remmington."

"Right, but I'd say that too." I stuffed the letter into the envelope and sent it to a secret location with a flick of my wrist. "Who would pretend to be Gabe and who would pretend to be Dexius? And why? Why would someone do that?" I stood, put everything else back where I'd found it, and headed back to the car.

"To keep you from doing what you're doing. Dexius probably morphed into Gabe all those times, and he probably found some poor guy, made him a replica of himself, and then shot him. He's evil. I wouldn't put it past him."

"But why would he shoot the guy?"

"If he's evil, he doesn't need a reason."

"I need to talk to Kaedan. He'll know what to do."

In the car, Cooper said, "Gabe said not to trust anyone."

"No. He said to watch who I trust, and if he's watching me, he knows about Kaedan. If he didn't want me to trust him, he'd say so. That means I can." I tapped my fingers onto my steering wheel. "What if that's a lie too? What if it's not Gabe who wrote those letters?"

Cooper climbed onto the dashboard. "That's what I said before, and you disagreed. What changed your mind?"

"Because I've been tricked over and over again. I don't know what to believe anymore."

"You're right. You have been tricked repeatedly, but I've changed my mind. I believe it's from Gabe."

"You can't— " I turned toward him. "Wait. Why? What do you know?"

"It's my job to protect you. When something isn't right, sometimes I get this funky feeling in my paws. Like they're falling asleep, and I can't feel them."

"Really? When have you had it?"

"Not recently, well, yes, recently because I have it now, which is weird. Okay, it doesn't happen often, but when it's the opposite, when something is good, that happens a lot. I'm about ninety percent accurate. The letter is from Gabe. I can feel it in my soul."

I had no other choice but to believe Cooper. He was my

familiar, and his sole job was to do right by me. If I could trust any living being in the world, it was him. But that didn't mean I would stop searching for Gabe. It simply meant I'd switch gears. Instead of looking for him outright, I'd figure out who'd posed as him and who dropped fake Dexius in my apartment to almost die. The answers to those questions would lead me to Gabe. They had to.

∼

My doorbell rang. I peeked through the peephole and saw Remmington standing there, a toothpick in his mouth again. What was up with them? It was the third time he'd had one. I unlocked the locks. "Did you find anything?"

He opened the door wider and stood against it. "Only these two file boxes."

Remmington had Gabe's MBI case files as well as the ones from the Holiday Hills Police Department. He'd been a real trooper helping me. The guilt about Remmington hit me like a brick. Gabe knew. I wasn't sure I'd ever forgive myself for that. And I wasn't sure I'd ever forgive myself for encouraging Remmington's help with my search for my former significant other when I still had feelings for him. I stared at the box and then at him. "How did you get the MBI files?"

"I know some people there."

"Wow. Good. But, seriously? That many?"

"Gabe's a good cop. He made a lot of arrests, and when that happens, people are bound to be mad."

I motioned for him to come in, then flicked my hand, and the boxes appeared on my coffee table. "So, basically, Gabe's ticked off a lot of people."

"A lot of bad people, Abby. You sure you want to do

this?"

"I don't have a choice. Someone is messing with my life, and I need to stop them."

"Are you sure this isn't something more?" A wine bottle appeared in one of his hands and two glasses in the other. He set down the glasses, popped open the wine, and poured it for us.

I took a glass and opened a box after sitting on my couch. "It's about a lot of things, Remmigton." I watched his curious expression switch to resignation. He sat next to me.

"Well then, let's get started."

"If I do find Gabe, I can't make any promises. Do you understand that?"

"You're saying you still have feelings for Gabe." He faced me. "I've known that all along, and I've willingly taken the risk. I'm not stopping anytime soon."

"Good one," Cooper said from behind the couch. He climbed onto the couch's back. "This dude is good."

I didn't know what to say, and blurted out, "Shall we get started?"

"Yup."

Cooper jumped from the couch and sniffed around my apartment, his nose to the ground as if he were on a mission. His nearly bionic nose led him to Remmington. He smelled his leg and then jumped back. "That's weird."

I shifted my eyes toward him.

"Ask him about the vision," Cooper said.

"What?" I asked.

"Just do it, Abby, please," Cooper said.

Remmington grinned at me. "I didn't say anything."

"Sorry, I was just thinking out loud." I stood and stretched. I stared at the glass of wine and realized I didn't want it. "I'm getting a water. Would you like one?"

"You don't want to drink your glass of wine?"

"Not really. I'm sorry."

"Don't be sorry."

"You sure you don't want a glass of water as well?"

"No, thanks. I'm good."

I ambled toward the kitchen, signaling for Cooper to follow. "What vision thing? What are you talking about?"

"He smells funky."

"He worked all day. He probably hasn't showered."

"Not that kind of smell," Cooper said. "It's something else. I can't explain it. Just ask him about the vision thing. You know, it's mine to see thing? That one."

"Do you think it's Kaedan in disguise?"

"I'm not sure. I just know something's not right."

"There's no possible way Kaedan would disguise himself as Remmington and not tell me."

"Humor me then," he said.

"Fine, but I think this is ridiculous."

"Let's hope you're right."

I grabbed a glass of water and casually sat beside Remmington. I couldn't just say the phrase without any context. He'd have no clue what I was talking about. Then again, wasn't that what I wanted? "So," I said, flipping through another file. "The vision is mine to see."

Remmington glanced up from the paper he'd been reading. "What?" He hadn't changed into Kaedan.

"The vision. It's mine to see."

He raised an eyebrow. "Is that something in the file?"

I narrowed my eyes at Cooper then smiled at Remmington. "Nope. It's just something stuck in my brain. Kind of like an earworm, I guess."

"I get those sometimes," he said. "They drive me crazy."

"Right?"

He hadn't even flinched when I'd said it. If Kaedan had disguised himself as Remmington, he would have acknowledged it. I couldn't imagine a reason he wouldn't, so I wasn't worried. Cooper's nose was just out of whack.

We read through a quarter of the files until I found the first of three possible suspects.

"Jasper Cronin sounds like a real winner," I said. "He was on the MBI most wanted list for two years before Gabe arrested him. He murdered three witches. He's in jail now."

"Is he a warlock?"

"Said he wanted to eliminate anyone with greater powers than his." I shuddered thinking about what that could mean for Gabe. "Wait. He's out. How would he get out after murdering three witches?"

"He probably made a deal and gave someone up. It happens more often than you think."

"That's terrible," I said.

"Isblock Handdefur," Remmington said. "Also murder, but five. All warlocks. All deemed below him."

"Who deemed them below him?" I asked.

"According to the file, Isblock himself."

"Wow," I said. "That's scary."

He removed the toothpick from his mouth and set it on the table, then dug into his pocket and unwrapped another one and stuck it in his mouth.

"What's with the toothpicks these days?"

"Nothing. They're cinnamon flavored, that's all. Keeps my breath fresh." He removed another one from his pocket and handed it to me. "Try it."

"No, thanks. I thought you didn't like cinnamon?"

"What makes you think that?"

"Didn't Bessie offer you a cinnamon latte? I heard you said something about cinnamon bothering your stomach."

"Oh yeah. I wasn't in the mood for a cinnamon latte. I just didn't want to hurt her feelings." He looked at the information on Isblock again. "He's currently doing time in a magical high security prison, but that doesn't mean he's not our guy."

"The last one, Raphael Weeblet. Warlock. Theft by taking."

"Theft by taking? Is that a real thing? It doesn't sound MBI worthy," I said. "What did he take?"

"He stole the main magical computer chip from the MBI."

"Oh, that's a big deal."

"It is," he said. "His charges were reduced from various other, more serious ones."

"Why?" I asked.

"Because he was diagnosed with a disorder that affected his decision-making skills. He was released from a magical psychiatric hospital six months ago."

"So, one is still locked up and two are out. Looks like we know where to start."

A knock on my door startled me. I held up a finger and pressed it to my lips. At the door, I peeked through the peephole. "Oh, it's you," I said, and let Kaedan in.

"That sounded almost insulting."

"Are you okay? Your eyes are bloodshot."

"I'm fine. Just tired." He stepped inside on unsteady feet.

I grabbed onto his upper arm. His muscles felt softer than they looked. That was odd. Why would he portray firm muscles and let me touch them if they weren't real? "You sure?"

"Yes, I'm sure, but thank you for being concerned."

Cooper scurried over and rubbed his legs against Kaedan's ankles. "Whoa. My nose must be off kilter or something. I'm smelling the same funky scent everywhere lately."

"Come sit," I said. "You really don't look that great."

"Yes, ma'am." He noticed Remmington. "Long time no see."

"Wait," I said. "You two know each other?"

"We've worked a case or two together in the past," Remmington said.

I tilted my head to the side. "How? Where?"

"Special assignment through the MBI," Kaedan said. "Last year, I think."

Remmington nodded.

I was miffed. "You said you knew people at the MBI, but never told me you worked with them."

"It wasn't a big deal, Abby. I guess I didn't think to mention it."

"It is a big deal, Remmington. It instills trust. Is that how you got the files? You weren't honest with me."

"I was honest. I just didn't give you all the information, because I didn't think it was necessary. You still can trust me."

Cooper had climbed onto the back of the couch, but quickly jumped off and skirted into the bedroom. "I'm staying out of this disaster," he said as he used his backside to shut the door behind him.

"I'm following the cat," Kaedan said. "Call me back after the discussion."

"Wait," Remmington said. "Check on these names for me, will you?" He gave him the names he'd mentioned earlier.

Kaedan rolled his eyes. "Sure, friend." He disappeared less than a second later.

I glared at Remmington. "How dare you withhold that

from me?"

He tilted his head to the side. 'Why are you making a big deal about this? It was a year ago, maybe more. It just didn't cross my mind, and it didn't even involve your *boyfriend*, so why would it matter?"

His accentuation of the word boyfriend stung, but I deserved it. I made a loop around my couch. "I'm sorry."

"I know. I understand we can't move forward if you don't find Gabe, but I really wish you'd drop this. Not because I don't want to lose you, though, yeah, that's part of it. I don't want you putting yourself in danger. Let me handle things. I'll work with Kaedan. If anyone can find Gabe, it's us."

I appreciated the intention. "I'm not going to stop. I can't. You need to know that about me. When I put my mind to something, I follow through. It's who I am, Remmington. If you can't accept that, maybe you should move on."

"I wish you'd reconsider."

"Even if I wanted to, I can't. Gabe's left me messages. Look." I called for Gabe's note. When it appeared in my hand, I gave it to Remmington to read.

Before he finished the short note, Kaedan reappeared. "They're where they're supposed to be. No escapes or disappearances."

"What about the witch killer?" I asked.

"Back in the joint for killing a shifter."

I ran my hand through my hair. That was a dead end. Everything was a dead end. "Thanks," I said.

He glanced at Remmington who had an unusual scowl on his face as he read Gabe's notes, then looked back at me, and mouthed, "Everything okay?"

I shook my head.

"I'll talk to you later," Kaedan said and disappeared again.

Remmington finished and looked at me. "He didn't cast the spell?"

I shook my head. "That's probably why it faded so quickly."

He exhaled, rubbed his hand through his short hair, and said, "I'm not sure what to say."

"Ditto."

"Are you sure this is real? Maybe Dexius wrote it to distract you? Or maybe he's toying with you. Playing games. I don't know Gabe that well, but he doesn't strike me as the kind of warlock who'd go on a mission and not give his all."

My eyes narrowed. "What does that mean? Of course, he's giving his all."

"Then why would he be checking on you?"

"Because he's worried about me. He knows something's going on here. He can do both, Remmington. Put his all into a mission and keep an eye on the people he cares about. And have you forgotten he's a warlock? He could have sent the note here magically and made sure I'd find it. He didn't have to be here physically."

"Okay. I'm sorry. I shouldn't have said that." He stepped close to me, looked me in the eye and asked, "Do you have feelings for me, Abby? Real feelings?"

I swallowed and nodded. "I care about you."

"That's not an answer."

"It's not a no, but that's the most I can offer you right now."

"Then I'm in this," he said and then kissed my cheek. "Promises or no promises. But you have to trust me. I'd never hide anything from you. I promise you. I'll see you soon, okay? Please, don't do anything without coming to me first. At least do that for me, okay?"

"I'll try." Could I trust Remmington? I was so confused.

10

"It's late," Bessie said. "Is everything okay?" She'd answered the door in her garden gnome pajamas and a dark green bathrobe. She'd curled her hair around the old-fashioned brush-roller curlers my mother used to wear. My mother had put them in my hair when I was a child. Resting my head on the pillow made the curler bristles press into my head like a million needles, and I hated needles. I begged for her to take them out, and she did. How they slept on them, I'd never know.

"I don't know who else to go to."

She opened the door farther. "Come on in. I'll make coffee."

We sat in her family room. Not only had she made coffee, she also gave Cooper some leftover tilapia she'd made herself for dinner.

He drooled into the bowl. "Dear Goddess, this is the best fish I've ever had. Is that paprika I taste?"

"It sure is," she said.

Cooper muttered an, "It's amazing," with a mouthful of fish.

I didn't dare ask him to elaborate on how he knew the taste of paprika. I preferred pretending he'd always been a cat, but I knew that wasn't the case. Familiars could be animals only, but some had been human or even a magical in a past life. Usually, those had died at the wrong time, not their destined time of death, and the powers that be gave them the option to live again as something powerful. I wasn't sure I'd do it, but that was just me.

Mr. Charming snoozed on a blanket on Bessie's dining room table. He'd stayed with me for some time after my mother passed, and I knew, outside of a traumatic event concerning his magical, nothing would wake the bird. Even his own train-like snoring.

I explained the situation to Bessie and showed her the note.

"Oh, dear. This is a tough one."

"I know. I just don't know what to do."

She set the letter down on her coffee table. "I think you can trust Remmington. He's a good man, and I know he cares about you."

"But I barely know him."

"Abby," she said. She leaned toward me and moved a loose hair that had attached itself to my eyelashes. "Sometimes you have to take a leap of faith."

I shook my head. "I don't think I can do that, not knowing I still have feelings for Gabe."

She shrugged.

"And he wants me to stay out of this. He said he'd work with Kaedan, but Bessie, something feels wrong. I just can't figure out what it is."

"I don't know either. Do you trust Kaedan?"

"I think so. I'm not sure."

"Then let's do a little magic and see what comes up,

shall we?" She waved for a candle across the room, and it flew to her. She blew on it, bringing the flame to life. It flickered back and forth. "Oh, one and all, we come to you, curious and worried. Is he trustable, or should Abby scurry?"

Cooper rolled onto his back and groaned. "That tilapia. To. Die. For."

The flame flickered faster. As it did, a shadow appeared in front of us, covering Cooper with darkness. He jumped up onto his hind legs and stuck out his stubby little front paws. "What's that?"

"Shh," I said.

The shadow formed into a woman with dark hair cascading down her front, nearly reaching her waist. She wore a white toga-like dress. I wasn't sure what to do, so I just sat there.

"Trust is not something to be given generously, but when you do, it should be with caution, always." The woman smiled, then disappeared.

Bessie sighed. "Well." She made a tsk sound. "I'm sorry. I thought that would go better than that."

"Who was that? And what did she mean it should be given with caution? Is she saying I shouldn't trust Kaedan or that I should?"

"She's an elder witch. They always talk in circles, but that was the worst I've heard in years."

"So, can I trust him?"

Bessie patted my hand. "I think she's saying you need to decide for yourself."

"I'm not sure I can do that."

"Sometimes we have to learn lessons, and sometimes it happens the hard way."

I stuck out my bottom lip. I wanted easy answers. I

wanted the mountain man banished forever, and I wanted Gabe home safe. "That's not helpful."

"Just watch your back. If you feel Kaedan isn't doing right by you or Gabe, walk away. That's the best I can say, given the circumstances." She hugged me. "Sweet girl, your mother would be so proud of you."

"Thank you."

"Soon, this will all be a distant memory. Just let what is to be, be."

"That's not possible. I'm not wired that way."

"I figured. Neither was your mother."

I left her to get back to sleep and transported myself and Coop back to my apartment.

Kaedan was there when we popped in. He caught me by surprise. "What are you doing here? You can't just sit in my home while I'm not here. That's inappropriate and creepy."

"I just didn't want anyone else to see me."

I mumbled, "Fine," under my breath.

"Did you get things worked out with Remmington?"

"Sort of." I called for Gabe's note again and gave it to Kaedan.

After reading it, he asked, "Where did you get this?"

"Gabe led me to it. In a roundabout way."

"Are you sure it's from him?"

I fell onto my couch and sighed. "It's the only thing I'm sure of." Though I wasn't quite sure that was the truth. I was too confused to be certain of anything.

∾

STELLA MET me at the Enchanted the following morning. I'd barely slept thinking of how to connect with Gabe as well as other options I had or hoped to have had. Kaedan stayed late, but it was beneficial. He'd brought top secret MBI files I should have never seen, ones Remmington hadn't, and I was grateful. Maybe trusting him was the right thing to do? I learned details about Gabe that surprised me, upset me, and made me proud, but nothing I thought would lead me to him. I'd been a hot mess of emotions the rest of the night, thinking about the investigations Gabe had participated in, and how often he'd put his life on the line to save our magical and human societies. I asked Kaedan to do a double check on the three names I'd found in Remmington's files, and he promised to get back to me the next morning.

I spent the night thinking up plans to find Gabe, but what I came up with wasn't much.

When my mother was upset with someone, she'd tell me she had a bone to pick with them. Little did I know at that time, even though it was just a saying, she meant it literally.

After her death, I asked Bessie what my mother meant. She told me when my mom had a concern about a magical, she would use the magic of the forest to lead her in the right direction. I knew forests carried their own special kinds of magic, but I'd never seen it. I'd planned to find a bone and a forest magical because I had a bone to pick with Dexius, and I needed help.

Stella waved her hand in front of me. "Hello? Earth to Abby."

"Oh, sorry. Lost in thought."

Mr. Charming flew over and landed on my head. "Dyn-o-mite!" He plopped down onto the table and blew Stella kisses. "Hmm, kisses. Mwah! Dyn-o-mite!"

Bessie rushed out from the kitchen and held her arm out for the bird, but he didn't jump up. He just kept repeating the strange phrase. "Mr. Charming! We don't interrupt the ladies when they're having a private conversation."

He hopped toward her. "Oh, come on, Ma!"

Stella laughed. "Wow. What is that all about?"

Bessie blushed. "He was up all night after you left," she said to me. "Watching an entire season of *Good Times*, a TV show from the 70s."

He hopped onto her arm. "Van Gough, and Rembrandt, don't be uptight, cause here comes kid dyn-o-mite!"

"Oh, for the love of Goddess," Bessie said. She kissed his beak. "You're too much."

Stella laughed again. "Well, now that Bessie's stopped the threat of an explosion, let's talk about you. Why have the dark circles under your eyes doubled in color?"

I wanted to tell her the truth, but instead, I made up something silly. "Cooper was sick all night. Neither of us slept."

Cooper popped his head up from the chair and rested it on the top of the table. "Why are you throwing me under the bus? I slept like a baby."

I cleared my throat. "It happens every once in a while." I'd said that to Stella, but hoped Cooper got the message. "Too much tilapia with spices."

"Spices? Oh, yuck," she said. "That couldn't have turned out well."

"It wasn't all that bad," I said.

"You do know cats like to get revenge, right?" he asked.

I ignored him and listened to Stella making plans for the weekend.

"I'd love to go to that big indoor farmer's market in Atlanta." She pursed her lips. "I can't remember the name of it, but it's the one with all the seafood lying on the ice and staring at us." She shuddered. "The rest of the place is great, but I can't eat something that's looked at me, even if it's dead."

Cooper's eyes lit up. "Seafood? I'm in!"

I laughed. Stella loved animals, except exotic birds because they freaked her out. She should have been vegan, but she couldn't turn down a hamburger if her life depended on it. "It's the Dekalb Farmer's Market, and I'd love to go." I hoped a trip outside of my drama would improve my mood. "Let's plan on it."

She clapped. "Yay! They have this boysenberry jam that's to die for. It's a drive, so we'll leave at what, maybe nine on Saturday?"

"Perfect." I tapped my pencil on the table. "What's your plan for today?"

She heaved her bag from the floor and placed it on the table. She removed a large bundle of copy paper. "This."

I ogled the stack of papers. "Is that a manuscript?"

"Yup. All four hundred seventy-two pages of it. Not even double-spaced."

"New author?"

"Her maximum word count for this story is supposed to be 60,000 words. This baby is at least 200,000."

I grimaced. "Ouch."

"Since she sent it to me like this, I'm going to use a red ink pen. And I told her I needed a digital copy as well."

"Did you tell her you don't accept paper copies?"

"I did, but..." She smacked the manuscript with her hand. "She didn't seem to care."

Cooper's disinterest was evident in his sigh. "I'm going to Bessie. I need sustenance. Must be from getting so sick last night." He hopped off the chair, his thick, muscular body making a thump sound as his feet hit the ground. Without a backward glance, he sauntered to the kitchen.

"Did she send the digital copy?"

"Not yet, so just in case, I'm upping my fee," she

smacked her hand on top of the manuscript again. "Antiquated process. She'll pay it, or she won't get it back."

I laughed. "I don't know how you do it. I know how high maintenance I am as an author, and I wouldn't want to deal with me."

"You have your moments."

Kaedan walked in dressed as he'd been the night before. What happened to being undercover, I wondered. "Ms. Odell, a moment if you will."

Stella's neck twisted to get a look at Kaedan. When she whipped it back around, she was smiling and wide eyed. "Oh, my," she whispered. She fanned her face with her hand. "Oh, I'm just leaving," she said as she quickly stuffed the monstrosity of a manuscript back into her bag. "Pages to read. Literally." She blew me a kiss. "Have fun."

If only she'd known the truth.

Kaedan sat. "I don't have any more information on the three files you requested." He leaned back in his chair and placed his ankle on the opposite knee. "Care to tell me this idea of yours?"

If Dexius was somehow involved with any of those cases, say perhaps he'd disguised himself as one of the men, then I'd draw him in, and maybe I could get him to lead us to Gabe. "I've got a bone to pick with Dexius, and those three files are how I'm going to do it." If I could locate an area in a forest where Dexius had murdered one of his victims, then maybe getting a bone from that area would get me extra special information. It was a long shot, but it was all I had at that moment.

He peered at me intently and shook his head, asking, "Am I missing something here?"

I held out my hand, and he handed me the files. I

plucked the one I wanted first and quickly scanned through the updated information. "This is perfect."

"What's perfect?" Kaedan asked.

"I'll fill you in when we get there." I gathered my things and stuffed them into my bag.

Cooper sensed my desire to leave and rushed out from the kitchen. "I was just finishing up. Can't you give me some time to digest? Tuna's heavy on the digestive system."

"Stay. I'm going to the woods for a bone. I can meet you at home later."

Kaedan's eyes widened. "A bone?"

"I'm going with a no to that," Cooper said. "I know what you're doing, and sending a witch into the woods alone is just asking for trouble. With this extra tuna in the tum, I don't think I could get there from here fast enough if you needed me. So, let's go get this bone. I'm very good at finding lost items, by the way. Did I ever mention that?"

"Not that I can think of. While I appreciate the offer to help, this bone isn't lost. I think I know right where to go."

11

Cooper suggested I wear a red coat. I didn't find that funny. "I'm not Little Red Riding Hood."

"This is the mountains of North Georgia. These woods are filled with bears, bobcats, and wild hogs. Witch or not, I don't see you winning a fight with a wild hog."

"You weigh exactly nine pounds. You think you can win a fight with a wild hog?"

"In a hot minute, absolutely."

"Define hot minute," I said. I'd stopped my car just inside the entrance to Amicalola Falls, a touristy, forested area for hikers and campers filled with enough wildlife to stock a zoo.

"Oh, forget it," he said. He knew I wasn't going to do things his way, no matter what sass he threw at me, and Coop could throw a hefty dose of sass.

Kaedan stepped out of the car disguised as a backpacker. His short hair had grown down his back, and he'd styled it into dreadlocks. He'd grown a beard to the middle of his chest and wrapped the tip of it into a braid. I smirked, then covered my nose. "Oh, yuck. Did you have to add the skunk smell?"

"I thought it would be funny."

That was the first time he'd shown any real sense of humor. I glanced around the area. "Please, please change back. Just put on a baseball cap. No one here will recognize you."

"What happened to your sense of humor?"

"How would you know I have a sense of humor?"

He blinked. "Everyone has a sense of humor."

"Please, just change back. I prefer dealing with your real self."

"I'd rather not take the chance. It's too dangerous."

I sighed. "Fine." I reached for Cooper and held him close, then asked Kaedan to place his hand on my free shoulder. "Here we go." I flicked my wrist, giving my hand a swirl, and said, "Remove this smell from me alone, and send us straight to the desired bone." I breathed in deeply and smiled. "Much better."

We instantly appeared in a clearing on the top of the mountain near the waterfall away from the other visitors. I set Cooper on the ground. "Do you see it?"

He dashed off to the left. We jogged to keep up. He quickly stopped next to a tall pine tree with its lowest branches snapped off and began digging. A second later, he twisted his neck toward me, and said, "Little help here?"

"Back up, please." I flicked my wrist after he made room between him and the area. The ground shook as the small spot where Cooper had been digging opened and revealed a single bone. I couldn't determine what it was or what it was from, but I knew it had been in these very woods when that animal was still alive, and that was what mattered. I examined it carefully. "Watch out mountain man. I'm on your back now."

We settled at a small picnic table a reasonable distance from a group of hikers who were eating. Cooper's nose wiggled on high speed. I shook my head. "There is no way you can be hungry right now."

"I'm not. It just smells scrumptious." He walked over the files, leaving little paw prints on them as he did.

Kaedan tapped his fingers on the table. "Care to tell me what's going on now?"

"Sure," I said. I eyed his tapping fingers. "Stop that, and I'll explain."

He sat. "I'm impressed. I think."

"Don't be. This place was mentioned in a file you brought. I thought it was a long shot, but worth it. So, when my mother had problems with another magical, she'd find bones in the areas where that magical had been, and if they were in a forest, the forest magicals would give her information that helped her handle the individual she was having trouble with."

He furrowed his brow. "You know most forest magicals can't be trusted."

"That's not always the case."

He rolled his eyes. "Abby, this is too much. I'm fine with going out on a limb to bring Gabe home, but fetching a bone? That's a little ridiculous even for a magical."

"That's fine." I crossed my arms over my chest. "Feel free to leave. I can do this alone."

He closed his eyes and let out an exasperated sigh. "No. I'll stay." A small bug flew by his head. He swung his arm up and whacked it.

The bug said, "Ouch, that hurt," as it fell to the table.

I glanced down at it. It wasn't a bug. It was a forest magical. A fairy. I pointed to her. "Kaedan, it's a fairy!"

He studied her closely. "Abby, fairies can be very dangerous. Even the MBI keeps clear of them when we can. Let's go."

I dug my heels into the dirt below the table. "I'm staying."

The fairy shook herself, then buzzed up to Kaedan's eyes and said, "That wasn't nice," in a high-pitched voice.

"I'm sorry," he said. "I thought you were a bug."

She flew away.

"Wait," I yelled. "Aren't you here to help us?"

Kaedan tilted his head to the side. "I don't think that's a good idea. Let me just remind you, Gabe told me he wants me to keep you safe, and I read the note. He wants you to stay out of this. Let me cast the spell and handle Dexius."

"Could we just stop with that, please? I know what Gabe wants, but like I told Remmington, I'm not going to stop. I can't. So, can we just let it go and move on already?"

Cooper turned Kaedan's direction. "She doesn't play around."

I stared at Kaedan. "You can hear him? The only other person I know who hears Coop is Bessie." A brick settled in the pit of my stomach.

His eye twinkled. "I said I'm like a high priest. Did you not believe me?"

"I believe you."

"Good, but no, I can't hear him, though I can tell when he's talking to you by the microexpressions on your face."

"Really?"

"Yep."

I'd had no idea I even made microexpressions. "Anyway, can we just move on?"

"I guess," he said, but it was obviously under duress.

"Good, then it's settled." I set the bone on the table, brushed off the dirt, and then whipped up a spell hoping the fairy would return.

The bone levitated from the table as I hastily encircled us with a protective, private bubble just in case. Sparkles framed it as it hovered over the table, and little rays of light gleamed from its sides. Cooper meowed and backed away, but I was mesmerized, transfixed by the beauty emanating from it. The lights, the sparkles, it was all stunning, and I couldn't wait to see what happened next.

But the thrill died as quickly as it began. The lights faded as the sparkles fizzled out. The bone trembled as it floated in the air before falling back onto the table. A fog surrounded me. I lost focus as a dizziness washed over me, threatening to suck me deeper into the fog. I tried to speak, but I couldn't. My body heated until my skin burned. I thought I was on fire, but I couldn't do anything about it. I was trapped, fully conscious, in agonizing pain, but unable to move. I attempted to scream again, but nothing came out.

What was happening to me? Would I survive? Was it Dexius? Was he hurting me?

The fog disappeared. For a brief second, I glimpsed Kaedan and Cooper sitting there chatting like old friends. I couldn't understand why they weren't alarmed or trying to help me. They disappeared again as the table began to spin. Terrified I would fall, I tried to grip the table, but my hands wouldn't move. I screamed for help, but it fell on deaf ears.

The table abruptly stilled. I shook my body back to reality. Or so I'd thought. As the fog cleared, I saw that Cooper and Kaedan had disappeared. I searched for the people sitting nearby, but they were nowhere to be found either. In fact, the entire area was desolate. Not a bug in the sky, nothing making any kind of sound. Not even a forest magical.

I didn't understand. Where was I? Was it some kind of alternate universe? Was I in the past? The future? I told myself to get it together. Something was going to happen, and I needed to be ready.

I stood and glanced around the area again. Something moved in the distance, but I could barely see it. It made a soft buzzing sound that grew louder and louder. The fairy! She buzzed in front of me, her teeny eyes locked with mine. "There is much trickery going on! Things are not as they seem. Danger is close! Please, go!"

"Trickery? What do you mean? Is the danger the mountain man? Is he close?"

"The man you seek isn't weak. Don't be fooled. He's not who you think. Remember, sometimes enemies are our friends, and sometimes, they're more."

"Wait. Who are you talking about? Who is he?"

She began to fly away, then buzzed back around. "Go, Abby! Now!"

I squeezed my eyes shut and disappeared.

12

I appeared back in my apartment breathless and shaking. Cooper and Kaedan sat on the couch.

Cooper saw me and rushed over and sniffed my ankles. "Next time you mess around in the forest, keep me on your lap. I couldn't smell you anywhere. You scared one of my nine lives out of me. And I'm pretty sure I'm down to three lives now."

"Abby," Kaedan said. "What happened?"

"I ... the fairy... How did you get here?"

"No clue. It wasn't by my hand if that's what you're asking."

I chewed on my bottom lip, desperate to figure out what was going on. I was lost in thought when a knock on my door jarred me back to reality.

"Ab, it's Remmington. Are you home?"

I opened the door with a flick of my wrist. Remmington, dressed in a pair of faded blue jeans and a black t-shirt, held a pizza box in the air with his fingers. He appeared freshly showered as well. "I brought pizza." He looked at Kaedan. "Oh, hey."

I glanced down at my watch and then up at Kaedan. "Seven-thirty? How did that happen?"

"Again, I'm trying to figure that out too," Kaedan said. "But I think we'll get back to this later." He stood. "I'm not one to interrupt date night." He glanced at Remmington, shook his head, then whispered in my ear. "Women deserve better than cold pizza." He placed his hand on my shoulder. "I'll be back tomorrow, okay?"

"Okay."

"What's up with him?" Remmington asked. "You love pizza." He set the box on my coffee table.

"Nothing. We just had an eventful afternoon, that's all."

Cooper meandered to the pizza, gave it a sniff, and meowed his disapproval. "No anchovies." He stretched and yawned, then rubbed himself against Remmington's legs. "At least he smells normal again." He yawned again. "I'm exhausted. I think I'm going to give you two some alone time. Don't worry about feeding me. I'm not hungry." He shook his head. "Whoa. I don't think I've ever said that before."

I smiled as he sauntered into my bedroom and kicked the door closed behind him.

"You do look like you had an eventful day. Remmington examined me with squinted eyes. Through pursed lips, he asked, "What happened?"

I summoned a mirror and studied myself. My hair hung in knots as if a brush hadn't touched it in months. A long tear down the side of my shirt revealed my black lace bra. I pulled the shirt over to cover it and noticed dark stains on my pants. I was also missing a shoe. "Oh, my." I twirled my hand and magically became normal Abby, leaving the one who'd been through the ringer behind. "It was nothing," I lied. "We went for a hike and I fell, that's all."

"A hike? With Kaedan?" Remmington stepped toward me and lifted my chin to his face. "Are you okay?"

I nodded, then shuffled into the kitchen for plates and napkins. "I had an interesting experience," I said, then realized I shouldn't have said that. His questions would either force me to lie again or tell the truth, and I hated lying.

He placed a piece of pizza overflowing with veggies and meat onto my plate. I sat on the couch and took a bite. The warm, salty cheese oozed into my mouth, igniting my taste buds and sending waves of pleasure to my brain. Green peppers teased my tongue, and I stuffed two more bites into my mouth before taking a breath. "This is so good," I said after swallowing. "I didn't realize how hungry I was."

He sat next to me. "What's going on? I'm worried about you."

I didn't know what to say. Did I tell him about the fairy's warning? About the bone and how it almost led me to the mountain man? The fairy's words echoed in my head. *Don't be fooled. He's not who you think.* I leaned back into the couch cushion and yawned. "I went looking for the mountain man, but I didn't find him."

"Where did you go? Why didn't you ask for my help?"

"Because you have a job, and I had Kaedan."

He flinched. I hadn't meant to hurt his feelings, but I'd done that a lot, and intentional or not, it wasn't good. "I didn't mean it like that."

"I know. Did you learn anything?"

I shook my head and took another bite of pizza. Breaking every Southern manner in the book, having a man in my apartment alone, not wearing makeup around guests, wearing pants, I figured what damage could one more do, and spoke with my mouth full of the yummy food. "Nothing. It's like everything is a complete dead end. I need to find the mountain man. I know he'll lead me to Gabe." I didn't tell him what the fairy said. What if she'd been talking about him? What if he wasn't who I thought? And if that was true, what did it mean? Did it mean he was trying to hurt me? Trying to hurt Gabe? Had he sent the mountain man to torture me? I didn't know what to think. My lungs deflated. I curled my shoulders in. "Maybe you and I should, you know."

He dropped his head to the side. "Break up?"

We hadn't said we were exclusive, but I figured it was assumed. I just hadn't thought of us that way. "Just take a break until I figure this all out. I hate hurting you like this, Remmington."

He shook his head. "No, I know. It's okay. I'm not leaving you to deal with this alone. Whether we're together or not, I'm not going to let you do this alone." He took another piece of pizza and set it on his plate. "Now, tell me everything."

∼

"A FAIRY?" He leaned back into the couch. "Wow. I haven't seen a fairy since I was a kid. They don't like other magicals."

"You've seen one? She was my first."

He blinked. "One came to me before my first familiar died."

"You had another familiar?" Remmington's familiar kept himself invisible most of the time. I wasn't sure why, and when I asked, he just said he was a shy stallion. His smile dropped into a frown. "A pig. I'd named her Bertha."

"What happened to her?"

"She was poisoned. It's a long story, but it's why Royal prefers to stay invisible. Less risk."

"I'm sorry." I looked at my bedroom door and pictured Cooper all snuggled up and cozy between the pillows. I couldn't imagine what I'd do without him. "That must have been hard."

"I dealt with it." He shook his head as if he needed to clear his brain. "So, what did she tell you?"

I folded my legs up under me. "Just what I said, nothing else." I felt uncomfortable saying anything more.

He rubbed his forehead. "She showed herself to you for that?" He took a breath and added, "That's unusual."

His eyes showed such concern. I felt awful for lying to him. He'd done so much for me in such a short time. He'd taken Gabe's position as Holiday Hills police chief. He worked for the MBI. He'd never done anything to hurt me. I should have been able to trust him. I wanted to trust him, but all the warnings stopped me. I wasn't sure what to do. What if he was involved and I didn't know it?

"I know that look. I know you want to tell me, but you're worried. Let me help. Please."

On a whim I decided to trust him. He'd never given me a reason not to, even before we'd gotten involved romantically. "She said someone is not who I think and that sometimes our enemies are our friends."

"What does that mean, someone's impersonating someone else?"

Why would he have gone there? I'd thought the fairy meant someone who cared about me was only pretending, but I never considered someone might be impersonating someone who cared about me. What if it was Remmington? What if he was the one who didn't really care about me? No, I couldn't go there.

I just couldn't imagine that to be true, but the rock settling in my stomach said otherwise. "I don't know. She didn't say anything else." I wiped a tear from my eye. "I don't know what to do."

"Abby." He set his plate on the table and scooted closer to me. "Let's think this through. Why would someone impersonate Dexius? That doesn't make sense. Maybe she's trying to mislead you? Fairies don't like other magicals. You know that."

"I don't know, but something tells me she's right."

"Okay, let's say she was being truthful. Who do you think it could be? Has anyone acted out of character?"

"Out of character?" I closed my eyes and ran through the past few months, replaying my days, my conversations, everything. My eyes popped open. "There's one person."

He dropped his plate into his lap and leaned forward, his eyes wide and focused on mine. "Who?"

"Waylon." I sighed. "Obviously," I shook my head. "It can't be him. He's just different because he's in love with Bessie. It's not him."

"Did you ever think that maybe it's Kaedan," he asked. "He appears out of nowhere and says he'll help you find Gabe?"

"Actually, he told me to stay out of it, but then he changed his mind. He said Gabe asked him to watch over me."

"That's strange already."

"Maybe, but he said he'd help me find Gabe. Why would he do that if he wasn't a good magical?"

"I'm not sure, but if he's gone against his mission, which, according to what you just said, was to stop you from searching for Gabe, he's gone rogue. That's strange to me, going rogue to help another agent. Why would he put his job and his future on the line like that?" He shook his head, then set his pizza plate on the table and stood. "No. It's him. He's the mountain man. He has to be. He thinks hurting you will hurt Gabe."

I felt something nudging at the back of my brain. I squeezed my eyes shut, begging it to come forward, to make itself known, but it wouldn't. I sank into the couch. "I don't know. I'm confused."

"Then let's start at the beginning."

Remmington left hours later after we'd written down everything we knew about Waylon and Kaedan, which was really a whole lot of nothing. We couldn't think of any logical or magical reason Waylon would want to hurt me or Gabe, but still, the fact that he'd suddenly become nice and was involved with someone very close to me, gave me pause.

Kaedan, on the other hand, was even less of a success. I didn't know anything about him, and everything Remmington had been able to find out wasn't bad. None of it made sense.

I begged my brain to shut down, but it refused. Conspiracy theories flooded it. I turned on the TV hoping for a distraction and maybe a little snooze, and a TV show I'd watched a few years before played on the screen. *In Plain Sight*. And that's when I realized what had been nudging at the back of my brain.

Dexius was in Holiday Hills, hiding in plain sight. The fairy was right. He was pretending to be someone I knew. That had to be it.

13

Bessie held the Enchanted's front door open for me. "Bless your heart, you look exhausted. Let me make you something special."

I smiled at Mr. Calloway sitting in the comfy leather chair by the fireplace. Waylon normally sat with him, as did one other magical, Roger Jameson, but Waylon was busy with Mr. Charming, and Mr. Jameson wasn't there.

Mr. Charming saw Cooper and hopped off Waylon's arm to greet his pal. He ambled over, his little clawed feet click-clacking on the tile floor. "Coopie doopie do! Coopie doopie do!" He rubbed the side of his face against my familiar's side. "Mr. Charming loves Coopie doopie do!"

Cooper gagged. "He smells like strawberries." He gagged again. "You know I hate strawberries."

I held out my arm and called for the green parrot. "Come give me kisses."

He moseyed over. "Up. Up."

I crouched down, and he climbed onto my arm. He leaned his beak to my cheek and said, "Hmm, kisses. Muah! Muah!"

"Muah," I said back. "Abby loves Mr. Charming."

Waylon laughed. "The old bird knows how to charm the women, that's for sure."

Bessie patted Waylon on the back. "Hence the name Mr. Charming."

Waylon's shoulders hitched up and then back down. "To have that kind of appeal."

Bessie bounced onto her tiptoes and kissed him on the cheek. "You have it with me, and that's what matters."

Cooper gagged again. I shot him a glare. "I can't help it. Romance makes me ill," he said.

Sometimes I felt that way as well.

"Let me get you something special," Bessie said to me. "Waylon honey, sit with Abby and chat with her. She looks like she needs a friend, and Stella's already been here today."

"She has?" I asked. "That's a bummer."

"She'll be back later when she takes a break from the paper monster. That's what she called it."

"Ah, got it. Oh, nothing special in my drink please, Bessie. I have a lot going on right now."

Her eyes narrowed. "You sure? It might help."

"I'm sure, but thank you."

Waylon sat across from me. He sipped his coffee, looking up at me from the cup. "Bessie's told me some about what's going on with you. Any luck in your search for Gabe?"

"She told you? What did she say?"

He pressed his lips together and shook his head. "Oh, no. I'm sorry. She wasn't supposed to say anything, was she? Darn it. I didn't mean to get her in trouble. I just wanted to help. Don't be upset with her."

"I'm not upset with her. Bessie's family to me. I know

she'd never intentionally do something to hurt me." I stressed intentionally, hoping he'd get the point.

His expression didn't change. "No, of course not. She loves you like her own. That's why she's so worried about you." He set his cup down. "I might be an old warlock, but I've still got a few tricks up my sleeve. What can I do to help?"

It was as if Goddess had dropped a lead-in right into the conversation and right into my lap. "Did you know Gabe has a brother?"

"He mentioned it once a while back, but I got the impression they weren't close."

"What did he say?"

"We were discussing family. I said something about mine being hard to handle." He looked off toward the back of the bookstore. "You know, come to think of it, he really didn't say much. He just said he had a brother, and that was it."

"Did he call him by name?"

"No, Abby. He didn't."

"Did you two talk about anything else? Did he say anything about his relationship with his brother?"

He shook his head. "No. Not that I can remember."

I redirected the conversation hoping to find some hidden nugget in Waylon's words or body language regarding his true feelings for Gabe. "How do you feel about the way Gabe policed Holiday Hills?"

It was a micro-change, but I saw it. He grimaced before swapping it out for a wide-eyed, toothy smile. "Gabe was a great police chief. He did a lot for the community."

"Did you ever have a run-in with him?"

Mr. Calloway walked past on his way to the bathroom. He slowed as he reached the table. Was he snooping?

Waylon leaned forward and hitched his head to the side. "A run-in?"

"Yes. Like maybe you two disagreed on something?"

He leaned his back against his chair and laughed. "Me and Gabe? Not that I can think of. I might have been cantankerous over the years, but I respect the law and those who enforce it."

Bessie walked up with my coffee so I couldn't ask my next question. "Here you go, sweetie." She must have noticed my tight lips because she asked, "Are you okay?" She looked at Waylon. "Waylon Hastings, did you say something to upset Abby?"

He held his palms up in front of his face. "No, hon. I didn't. I swear. We were just talking about Gabe. That's all."

She stared at him. "And what did you say?"

He hung his head. "I told her you told me what's going on." He looked up at her with genuine shame in his eyes. "I'm sorry. I only wanted to help. I told her I liked Gabe. He was a good police chief."

I once watched a TV crime drama, one of those weekly shows with a continued storyline, and the main character, a detective, said something that stuck with me. I'd used it in my books many times. *A person who doesn't know or can't accept someone is dead speaks of that person in the present tense, but a person who knows that someone is dead, uses past tense.*

Waylon Hastings spoke about Gabe in the past tense.

Mr. Calloway walked by again. "Excuse me," I said to Bessie and Waylon. I stopped Mr. Calloway before he went too far. "Hi. Do you have a minute?"

"Sure. What can I do for you?"

Mr. Calloway was a shifter, but he only shifted at night, and when he was alone. I'd been wary of shifters when I first learned of magicals, but I've learned to appreciate them for their unique personality traits and limited magical abilities. Plus, I wasn't afraid of them anymore. My magic was top notch, and I knew I could outsmart a shifter if necessary.

I grabbed my coffee and stood. "Let's sit by the fireplace. I need to take advantage of the comfy chairs more often." I smiled at Waylon and said, "Thank you for talking with me."

His mouth fell open, but no words came out. As I walked away, he said, "Sure."

I heard Bessie whisper, "What did you say to upset her?"

I sat in the chair beside the one Mr. Calloway deemed his. His furrowed brow and squinted eyes told me he was curious but concerned about what I wanted to discuss.

"I wanted to talk to you about Gabe."

His eyes widened. "Gabe? Have you heard from him? Is he okay?"

In small towns, even though secrets were secrets, nothing was secret. "I haven't heard from him, but I've learned some things recently. I know you two talked often. Would you consider him a friend?"

He rubbed his white beard. "I wouldn't call us friends, but we were friendly. Gabe wouldn't share private information with me if that's what you're asking."

"So, you don't know about his family?"

"I know he's got a brother, but that's about it."

"Did he tell you that?"

"No, ma'am." He leaned onto the arm rest closest to me. "I heard Waylon and Remmington talking about it."

Waylon and Remmington talked about Gabe? Why hadn't Remmington told me? "Was this here?" Why hadn't Waylon mentioned it a few minutes before?

He shook his head. "We were at the pizza place down

the way. Remmington walked in to pick up a pizza to go, and Waylon walked over to him at the counter."

"How do you know they were talking about Gabe if you were at the table still?" I asked. The restaurant wasn't big, but the tables weren't close to the counter, and if the place was crowded, there was no way Mr. Calloway could hear them.

"I walked by to use the bathroom. Now, I'll admit, when I heard Gabe's name, I stood around the corner of the kitchen wall and listened. I know you and Remmington are an item now, and I wanted to make sure he wasn't spreading gossip."

"I appreciate that. What was said about Gabe's brother, and who said it?"

He twisted to the side and stared into my eyes. "Abby, is there something going on?"

I shook my head. "I'm just trying to fit the puzzle pieces together, you know? Everything's fine. I just have questions."

"Well, Remmington said Gabe would be hard pressed to find his brother because he knew how to hide in open places. I remember because it made me think maybe his brother is a shifter, but we know that's not possible."

"What did Waylon say?"

He rubbed his beard again. "I'm not sure I should tell you, Abby. I see Bessie and Waylon, and they look happy. I don't want to interfere."

That meant I needed to know. "Mr. Calloway, if Waylon is putting Bessie in danger, I need to know."

"No, no. That's not what I meant. I—" he exhaled. "Waylon doesn't like Gabe. In fact, shortly before Gabe left, he brought Waylon in for questioning. Waylon wasn't happy, and he told me they'd argued. Waylon said he'd make sure Gabe wasn't the police chief if it was the last thing he did."

"Did he tell you what they argued about?"

"No, and I didn't want to know. I try to stay out of the Holiday Hills gossip. The less I know, the happier I am."

I understood that. "Thank you, Mr. Calloway."

"Abby," he said as he leaned closer again. "I don't want you telling Waylon what I said, okay? I don't want to have to find a new coffee shop in another town."

"I won't." I decided to keep the secret and use it if needed, but through channels. "What about Remmington? Do you know him well?"

He peered into my eyes and raised his eyebrow. "That's an odd question to ask about someone you're involved with."

"I'm still getting to know him, and I'm taking it slow."

"I know he didn't get along with Gabe, and I know he forced the other chief out to get the job. I know he's got a poor reputation in other magical cities."

My eyes widened. That was a lot of things to know, especially for someone who didn't know Remmington all that well, and they were all news to me. "What? How do you know these things?"

He glanced at the door and then back at me. "I think it's best I stop there. Some things need to be seen on their own to learn the lesson." The corners of his eyes crinkled. "I've got to get going. You have a nice day, Abby." He walked to the front door and left.

How odd. Apparently, Mr. Calloway thought I had a lesson to learn, and he was right, but it probably wasn't the one he'd meant. I'd learned to not trust Remmington.

14

I sat at my pseudo worktable toward the back of the Enchanted trying to focus on the manuscript I needed to finish, but I was distracted by everything. Three teenage girls walked in. Giggling, they skipped past me and then darted to the book section on spell casting. I watched them flip through old, leather-bound books and new ones with fake witches and cauldrons on bright shiny covers. If they were witches, they would have known to stick with the older books, but they'd glued themselves to the newer ones. They probably wanted to cast a love spell. I smiled to myself. If they found something that worked, which was unlikely, they'd learn quickly that things don't always go as planned, especially when it came to spells. Love spells especially. They usually backfired and left the witch wishing she hadn't cast it.

But their search gave me an idea. I had a decision to make. Should I cast spells on Holiday Hills law enforcement officers to get information? Was that self-serving or was it to help Gabe? Normally, I would have asked Bessie what I should do, but I worried bringing her further into the situation would reveal things about Waylon better left unrevealed, at least for that moment.

If the fairy was right, and why wouldn't she be, Dexius was hiding in plain sight, likely disguised as someone close enough to stay one step ahead of me in my hot mess of a situation. As far as I knew, Remmington and Waylon were my best options, but I had to add Kaedan to the list since I really didn't know him well. If casting a few harmless spells on some unknowing humans gave me the information I needed, there couldn't be harm in that. Right?

I crammed my things into my bag, guzzled down the last of my cold coffee, and slipped into my jacket.

Cooper's left eye popped open. He'd been snoozing on the table in front of my laptop. "We going somewhere?"

"I have a plan."

"Oh, for the love of Goddess, what now? This is what, your tenth plan so far this week? Execution is key, Ab, but a good plan is most important, and so far, you haven't had any."

"Way to be supportive, Cooper."

He stretched before standing, then finally climbed onto the chair, and hopped onto the floor. "I am supportive. I could be partnered with a witch who fishes for a living, but nope. I'm with you. That right there is what I call dedication."

"You're right," I said. "And I appreciate everything you do for me, especially how you don't complain about any of it."

"Is that sarcasm?"

"Maybe." He followed me past the girls in the book aisle. I grabbed the old leather book of spells and headed to the front doors. "Bessie," I said, holding the book up and waving it back and forth. "I'm borrowing this. I'll have it back soon."

"No problem, sweetie. See you soon."

"Where are we going?"

"To the police department."

"You're dragging me along to go see your new boy toy?"

I cringed. "Don't be icky, and no. I'm going to cast a spell on some of the officers to find out about Gabe and Remmington."

"Oh, this will be interesting. But how are you going to do that without Remmington knowing?"

"Don't you worry. I have a plan." I unlocked my car, waited for Coop to jump in, then set my bag on the passenger seat. I watched Mr. Calloway walking toward the Enchanted. He stepped inside. "That's odd. He was there only an hour ago. I wonder why he came back?"

"Don't know," Cooper said.

I hollered to him. "Hey, Mr. Calloway, you forget something inside?"

He turned toward me. "Good morning, Abby. I'm getting a late start today. You have a good day." He opened the door and walked inside.

"That's weird." I stared at the door. "I wonder if he's ill?"

"He's old. Every living creature has memory problems when they're old."

I closed my car's door. "Hold on." I raced back into the Enchanted and over to Mr. Calloway.

"I was not," he said to Waylon.

"What's going on?" I asked.

Mr. Calloway's face was red. "This old man says I was just here minutes ago. I told him he's losing his mind."

I crouched down and met Mr. Calloway eye to eye. "Mr. Calloway, you were here. We just talked. You don't remember?"

He stared off into the distance. "I don't recall being here. Don't see how I could forget something like that."

Waylon patted him on the shoulder. "I forget a lot of things. It's rough getting old."

Mr. Calloway nodded.

I wasn't sure what was going on. I'd never seen Mr. Calloway forgetful to that level. Something didn't feel right. But then again, nothing had felt right since Gabe left.

I headed back to my car.

"He okay?" Cooper asked.

"He doesn't remember being there."

"That's weird."

"Or maybe he's up to something, and we don't know what," I said.

"Abby, he's not involved in Gabe's disappearance. You can't think that."

"I don't know what to think anymore." I opened the bag, removed my things, and sent them back to my apartment, then jammed the heavy book inside. I'd kept a pad of paper for notes. I called Remmington on my way over, which wasn't far, so I drove below the speed limit. "Hey, I'm at a place in my manuscript where I need some law enforcement help."

"Oh, I'd love to help, Abby, but I've got meetings all day."

"That's okay. I was hoping I could talk to some of the officers. The human ones would be great."

"Why not the magicals?"

"Because they can do anything they want, and it wouldn't be unrealistic in a magical book. I need a little help with the human law enforcement side to make it more authentic."

He chuckled. "Got it. Come on by. I'll get you set up."

"On my way, but can I pick who I talk to?"

"Absolutely."

I thanked him as I pulled into the parking lot. "Wouldn't Remmington be suspicious if he was really Dexius?"

"Maybe," Cooper said as I picked him up. "Maybe not."

"That's helpful." I took a deep breath and released it. "He didn't sound suspicious."

"In case you forgot, I'm here to protect you. I'm not a magical sleuth, so I can't read minds. Well, not any other than yours obviously."

"I know. You're a magical sleuth's sidekick."

"Good grief."

Before going inside, I marked the spell page in the book and set things up so the spell would work with every human officer I saw, without me having to repeat it.

Remmington set me up in a small conference room at the front of the department. While he had his assistant gather the officers I'd requested, I studied the conference room closely. I didn't see any cameras or recording devices, but a magical could use something invisible to other magicals, so just in case, I cast a protective spell to keep my conversations private. If Remmington was recording, and he was Dexius, he'd find out I was up to something, but that was a risk I was willing to take.

The first officer arrived. Steve Banks. He'd worked with Gabe, and they'd become friends over the years, even though Steve was still patrol. He was a nice guy, and it didn't hurt that he strongly resembled Ryan Reynolds. So much so, people asked for his autograph when he went into the city.

I gave him a tight hug. "Thanks for being willing to help."

He sat across from me. "This will be fun. My wife reads all your books, so she'll love that I helped."

I set the book of spells on the table. Keeping it closer to the officers was key to the spell working. "Great! I'll give her a paperback copy once I have them." I flipped to a clean page of my paper and started off with some random law enforcement questions to make sure the spell had time to work. They were always instantaneous, but I didn't want to take any chances. "When you've got a murderer on the loose, and you see his or her car on the road, how do you handle that? Do you call for backup?" Ugh, that was a silly question.

"We call for backup, maintain sight on the suspect, and wait until we have vehicles located near him to execute action."

"That makes sense," I said. "You and Gabe are close, right?"

His smile made his green eyes sparkle. "We are, yes. I hate that he's had to take this leave. We're all hoping he comes back soon."

Humans thought Gabe had a family issue out of the country. It was a weak cover, but it was Gabe's choice. "Yes, I'd like to have him back as well. Every police chief has enemies at work, so I'm sure Gabe was no exception. Is that your belief?"

"Even though Gabe is a great chief, he had his own for sure."

"Can you tell me who didn't like him?"

"Well, to start, the former interim chief. Thank God he's gone. And there's Ashford Mason, but he left before Gabe." He stared at the corner of the room. "You know, Gabe did a good job of getting rid of the ones he had issues with. The only one still here is Chief Sterling." He blinked. "I'm sorry. That's got to be strange for you."

He had no idea. "No need to apologize. Gabe and I decided to part ways amicably when he left," I lied. "What makes you say Remmington didn't like him?"

"Because he didn't. He'd tested to advance in rank several times. Passed the tests with flying colors, but Gabe wouldn't promote him."

"Do you know why?"

"Aside from a less-than-stellar reputation in the field, it was a simple lack-of-trust thing for Gabe. He once told me he thought something was off about Remmington, and he just couldn't trust him."

I wondered why Gabe didn't seem to disapprove about my relationship with Remmington then in his note. "Did he ever tell you what that something was?"

He shook his head. "I can tell you what I think it was though."

"Please do," I said.

His head shifted back and forth, then he leaned forward and whispered, "Chief Sterling's had a thing for you from the day he started in the department. Everyone knew it, but in the beginning, it wasn't a big deal. It became a big deal when he heard Chief Sterling talking about you."

"Talking about me? What do you mean?"

He glanced up at the top corners of the room. He wasn't a magical, and I hadn't seen any cameras in the room, so what was he looking at? "He heard Chief Sterling say he was going to take you away from him. Abby, Remmington has been in love with you since you moved back. Didn't you know that?"

My head spun. "He ... he ... no. That's not true. I didn't even know him until recently. That can't be possible."

"Love happens differently for everyone, and it looks like the chief, Sterling, I mean, had it bad for you. I even heard him talking about you right before Gabe took his leave. He's been planning a move on you for a while now, Abby. Are you sure you didn't know about this?"

I nodded so hard it gave me a headache. "I'm sure." My chest tightened. Why hadn't Gabe told me anything? What must those officers think of me? Almost the minute Gabe left, I was involved with a magical who'd promised to steal me from him.

"When you two began dating, he came to work the next day all smiles, and said he'd finally caught his fish."

My body stiffened.

Cooper noticed right away. "Oh, boy. She's going to blow!" He jumped off the table and darted under it.

I wasn't about to blow. I was already in the process, but I stopped myself from showing it as quickly as it had started. I dropped my pen and pressed the back of my forearms into the table. Locking them down would have been better, but I did what I could. "Fish?"

A blush heated up from his neck and covered his face. "I'm sorry. I shouldn't have told you that."

"No, Steve. I'm glad you did." I breathed through my nose to try and keep myself calm. "I need you to think, please. Are you sure Gabe didn't tell you anything else?"

He bit his bottom lip, then held up a finger. "Oh, wait. Gabe didn't say anything else, but there was a rumor he put Chief Sterling on leave the day he left, but the interim chief dropped it. I don't know if it's true though."

"Did you hear why he put him on leave?"

"Callahan said it had something to do with disrespect toward higher authorities."

That could have meant people above him at work or the magicals' bosses, and Steve wouldn't know anything about them. "How did Remmington become the new chief then?"

"He's not officially the new chief. He's still the interim chief even though he forgets that and tells everyone otherwise. He'd been cozying up to the mayor for a while from what I've heard. I think he was planning to push Gabe out."

I needed to process what I'd learned. Remmington wasn't the person I thought he was, and I wasn't sure how I'd deal with that. "Thank you, Steve. I really appreciate your help. Could you ask for Callahan to come in?"

"Sure thing." He stood. "I think using the chase scene I mentioned will take your book to the next level."

"I'm sure it will," I said smiling. The spell had given him memories of our meeting that I didn't have, but my book already had a chase scene in it, so he'd be thrilled.

I chewed down my longest fingernail waiting for Callahan to arrive. After fifteen minutes, the door opened, and I finally took a breath.

Only, it wasn't Callahan. It was Remmington. I plastered a fake smile on my face and acted excited to see him. Cooper stayed hidden near my feet. He hissed.

Remmington glanced under the table. "You okay, buddy?"

"He's been batting at a spider," I said. "He's probably just doing the cat version of pounding his chest to appear dominant."

Remmington patted his chest. "Does this make me dominant?"

"It makes you look funny."

He dropped his arms. "Callahan should be here any second. He's on his way back from a call. Do you need anything?"

I shook my head. "I'm fine. I thought you had meetings all day?"

"I'm heading into another one now." He leaned down and went to kiss me, but I turned my head to the side, and his lips landed on my cheek.

"Sorry," I said. "I had onions today."

"Got it," he said. He winked. "Dinner tonight?"

"I've got plans with Stella." I didn't, but he didn't need to know that.

"Okay. See you at the Enchanted tomorrow."

Callahan was opening the door as Remmington grabbed the knob.

"Hey, Abby. Long time no see." He met me on the side of the table, and we hugged. "How's it going?"

"Things are great," I said. Our eyes met. Callahan was taller than me, and I had to look up to make eye contact.

He furrowed his brow. "Are you okay?"

"Just tired," I lied. "This book is driving me crazy. That's why I'm here." I sat and moved the book of spells to my other side because Callahan sat next to me.

I watched as the spell did its job. His eyes softened, and he smiled. "Happy to help."

"Great. Was the rumor about Remmington being put on leave true?"

"Oh, yeah. Man, if Gabe knew he was interim chief, he'd be so mad. You know those two didn't get along, right?"

I exhaled. "Yes. Why was he put on leave?"

He angled his head to the left. "Didn't Gabe tell you any of this? Remmington told Gabe he was going to take you away from him. Said he'd do it if it meant eliminating him. It was bad, but no one knows the truth. They don't know what really happened."

"How do you know Remmington threatened Gabe then?"

"Because I was in the kitchen when he did. They were outside in the hall. They didn't know I was close by."

"Gabe didn't tell me any of this."

"Yeah, probably because he thought Remmington was

more of a nuisance than a threat. When Remmington told him that, Gabe laughed. That got Remmington all hot under the collar, and he said a few things no one should say to their boss, so Gabe put him on leave."

"Unbelievable." The fact that first Gabe, and then Remmington withheld all of that from me sent my blood pressure soaring.

"How did Remmington react when Gabe put him on leave?"

"He got mad, obviously. He threatened to make Gabe disappear right then and there. That just made things worse for Remmington. How he got the interim chief to keep him on stumps me though."

Cooper popped out from under the table and jumped onto my lap. I pet him while asking Callahan about Remmington's relationship with the mayor.

"I don't know for sure, but I think he's got something on him."

"The mayor has something on Remmington or Remmington has something on the mayor?" I asked.

"Remmington has something on the mayor. That's how he got the job."

15

Cooper and I headed straight home without me interviewing anyone else. I needed to process it all and come to terms with what I'd learned about the man I was dating. I changed into sweatpants and a baggy t-shirt, slipped on a fuzzy pair of socks, and then pulled a large sweatshirt over the t-shirt to warm me up. I made myself a cup of chamomile tea and fed Cooper a can of salmon I'd bought earlier in the week. While he ate and moaned during chewing breaks, I grabbed the bag of Oreos in the cabinet, dumped the tea, and replaced it with milk.

I sat on the couch dunking Oreos in the milk until they were soggy and falling apart, and then ate them. Cooper finished his salmon and stretched out above my head on the couch back.

"What if Dexius is posing as Remmington?" I asked.

"Wouldn't Gabe know that?"

"I don't know. Gabe's a powerful warlock, so Dexius probably is too. He could hide that, right?" I stuffed the fourth drenched cookie into my mouth.

"I don't know. But even if that's the case, you've got a bigger problem."

I finished chewing the soggy goodness, then said, "Bigger than Gabe being MIA and Dexius posing as Remmington? I can't imagine what that could be."

"It could be Dexius that's in love with you, and you could be the reason Gabe really left."

"Cooper! For the love of Goddess, don't even go there." I fought back tears. "The MBI sent him on a mission."

"That doesn't mean they weren't manipulated somehow. Dexius could have done something to make it happen. If he's as powerful as his brother, it's possible."

I set the cup of milk and bag of cookies on the table and sank back into the couch. "If any of this is true, this isn't love. It's obsession, and that's worse."

"And it would mean you've been kissing on Gabe's brother."

I dropped my head back onto Cooper. He rolled off the back of the couch. "Hey!"

I leaned over and said, "That's what you get for being snarky."

He jumped up and positioned himself on the couch cushion instead of its back. "I was just trying to lighten the mood."

"Well, it wasn't helpful."

"The thing is, Ab, if Remmington is just your regular run-of-the-mill warlock, and not Dexius, you've got an obsessed soon-to-be-ex-boyfriend, and still no idea of how to find Gabe or Dexius. Remmington may not be who you think, but either way, he's dangerous. You need to dump him before something bad happens."

He was right, but if I'd done that, I wouldn't be able to get the information I needed to find Gabe.

"Hey," he said. "We still have Waylon. He could be Dexius."

"I don't know. I'm just not seeing that. Besides, it would be horrible for Bessie."

He rested his little brown head on the cushion. "I know. Bessie doesn't deserve that."

"No, she doesn't. If he turns out to be Dexius, you'll see a side of me no one's seen."

"That does sound appealing, but I'd rather it be for any other reason. Bessie's happy. I want her to stay that way."

I picked him up and snuggled him. "You're a good magical, Coop."

He mumbled something into my shoulder, then forced his head out of my grip and turned it to the side. After taking a few deep breaths, he said, "You almost smothered me to death."

"Drama king." I set him back where he'd been. "I have an idea. Well, sort of."

"I think you've reached your limit of ideas, and I don't like where this is going."

"You never like where my ideas are going."

"There is that."

"Anyway, when my sleuth in my books can't figure out what's going on, and when she's asked questions that don't get her anywhere, she does some surveillance."

"I knew I didn't like where this was going."

"What other option is there? If he's Dexius, he's got to take a break at some point, right?"

"Who are we talking about here?" he asked.

"Waylon."

"But you just said you don't think he's the one."

"I know, but isn't a little sleuthy spying the best way to find out?"

"Do I really have a choice in the spying thing?"

"Nope."

"I didn't think so," he said. "If he's Dexius, and he's got a plan, he's going to follow that plan, Abby. He won't alternate between his real self and his host. He wouldn't take that risk."

My heart sank. I hadn't even thought of that. "Do you think he's taken over Waylon's or Remmington's bodies?" I swallowed back a lump forming in my throat and choked out, "Or worse?"

"Again, let's remember we're dealing with Waylon Hastings here, and I don't think he's our guy. But I do think whoever is doing this is either taking over the body of whomever he's impersonating, or he's disguising himself as that person."

"The only way to cross Waylon off the list is to watch him."

"Fine. Let's get this over with then." He stared at me. "You're going in that?"

I pointed my forefinger to the ceiling and twirled it. Instantly, my clothes changed to all black, ninja attire. "Better?"

Cooper glanced at his front paws and patted them together. "Seriously? You put me in a disguise too? Like a cat needs a ninja costume to spy on someone?"

"The most popular cat in Holiday Hills does."

He sat back and said, "I am quite the stud, aren't I?"

I flicked my wrist, and off we went.

We appeared outside of Bessie's home. I peeked into her family room window, and there she was, sitting on the couch with Waylon, his arm over her shoulders. My mouth dropped open, and then I said, "Oh, great."

"You're getting pretty good at that transporting thing," Cooper said.

"Are you being sarcastic, because I'm really not in the mood right now."

"Actually, I wasn't, and yes, I know that's probably a first. You said you wanted to go to Waylon, and here we are. Where he is. At Bessie's house."

"This isn't going to be helpful." I peered into the window again, and immediately ducked as Waylon stood and looked my direction. "Did he see me?"

"How should I know? I'm less than a foot tall."

"Cooper! I need you to be serious," I whispered. "Climb on my back and see what he's doing."

He did. "He's putting a jacket on."

"Thank God."

"Now he's lifting Bessie's chin. Oh, Goddess! Oh, Goddess! He's going to—" he climbed off my back and gagged. "He kissed her. It was awful! My eyes will never unsee that."

"Pause the hissy fit please and look again." Just then, the front door opened only a few feet from where we hid in the bushes. I made us invisible just as Waylon glanced our direction.

Bessie walked him down the front steps. "Really, don't worry about Abby. I'll talk to her. She'll be fine."

What was that about?

He smiled, kissed her on the cheek, and then got into his car before he promptly drove away. I watched as Bessie scrutinized the bushes where we hid. Thank Goddess, I'd made us invisible.

"Who's there?" she asked.

Or not. I held my breath.

She walked over and inspected the bushes. "I could have sworn I heard something."

Mr. Charming flew onto the front porch through the open door. "Mr. Charming loves Cooper. Mr. Charming loves Cooper." He flew right over to us and pecked me on my invisible cheek. "Muah! Kisses!"

"Abby? Is that you?"

I dropped my head back and groaned. After a flick of my wrist, we appeared standing in front of Bessie. "Yes," I said as I exhaled. I didn't know what else to say.

Her brows wrinkled. "What's going on?"

Mr. Charming waddled over to Cooper and rubbed his green face against Cooper's side. "Mr. Charming loves Cooper!"

"Please, bird," Cooper said.

"Abby? Are you okay?" Bessie asked.

There was no point in hiding it. I couldn't lie to Bessie. She'd been family to me. She was there for me during my mother's illness and after she died. She helped me adjust to my witchy ways. I owed her the truth, even if it hurt her, because that's what she would have done for me. "Can we come inside? I have something to talk to you about."

16

Explaining my theories to Bessie wasn't easy for many reasons, but mostly because while I did, she showed no emotion whatsoever. Not a brow flinch, a lip curl, a wide eye. She was the eagle waiting patiently for its next victim, and I was the fish swimming below him.

I finished with my extended explanation and waited for her to react. And then I waited some more.

Finally, she pressed her lips together and said, "The only way you're going to find out if Waylon is Dexius is if I help you. So, let's figure out what we need to do."

That wasn't the response I'd expected. "Uh, but..."

"Abby, you are my priority. I promised your mother I would look after you, and even if I didn't, you're family to me. Compared to you, Waylon is unimportant in the scope of my life."

"But I know you care for him."

"I do, but we both know his quick change from cantankerous to kind was strange, so it's quite possible he's Dexius. Don't worry. If he is, I'm prepared. I won't crumble like a cookie."

"Dang," Cooper said. "Bessie is the bomb."

"Thank you," she said.

Mr. Charming flew to his stand and perched on the second level. "Bessie is the bomb! Bessie is the bomb!"

I moved to the couch and sat next to her, leaning my head onto her shoulder. "I don't know what to do. It's bad if Dexius is either one of them."

"Are there any other options?" she asked.

"When I found out about Waylon, and then about Remmington, I stopped there. My gut says it's not Waylon, but I need to make sure."

"I agree. I'll tell you what. I'll start slow and talk to Waylon about Gabe. As a matter of fact, we were talking about him tonight as Waylon was leaving."

"I heard you mention me. Something about me being okay? Was that about Gabe as well?"

"Yes. Waylon is worried. He thinks Remmington is coming on a little strong, and he's worried it's confusing you."

"It was, but now, not so much." I moved from her shoulder to the end of the couch and pulled my knees to my chest. "Even if he's not Dexius, the things he's done are too much for me. I can't stay with him knowing what I know, and besides, he's been dishonest about basically our whole relationship."

"I understand."

"What did he say about Gabe?"

"That he should get in touch with you. He was upset that he hasn't made contact."

"If Waylon is involved, it's best he doesn't know any of this." Every ounce of my soul wished I didn't have to say the things I'd said, but I couldn't put the people I loved at risk any more than I already had. "Bessie, did you know Gabe brought Waylon in for questioning before he left?"

Her lip twitched. "He hasn't mentioned it. What was the reason?"

"Unknown still."

"I'll look into it."

Cooper had been doing figure eights between Bessie's coffee table legs. "Um, Ab? You forgot someone."

My internal notification dinged in my head. "Kaedan! Right. I was so focused on Remmington and Waylon, I forgot about the one magical who has all the capabilities to do this. Though I'm not sure why he would."

"Does he have a motive?" Bessie asked.

"I haven't quite figured that out."

"I've been suspicious of that magical from the start. Coming into my store in different disguises like he has. I understand he's got an important and secretive job, but all that fuss is a little over the top for my liking." She rubbed her eyes.

I reached over and gave her a hug. "I'm so sorry to throw this on you, but I didn't think I should keep it from you either. You're tired, and so am I. Let's regroup tomorrow, okay?"

"Sure thing, sweetie."

I picked up Cooper and disappeared. Only I didn't transport us home. I transported us to Waylon's.

"Really, Ab?" Cooper huffed when I set him on the ground. "Do you really think we're going to find out anything tonight?" He adjusted his kitty ninja outfit across his belly. "This thing is giving me a belly rash."

"Just a peek, okay? Then I'll destroy the outfit forever."

"Promise?"

I crossed my heart and studied Waylon's home. The one-story brick ranch was dark except for a dim light in the windows on each side of the front door. The smell of rotting wood lingered in the air.

"Fine." He peered at the home. "I'll take the right window. You take the left." He darted from the tree we'd been standing behind to one a few feet closer to the house. I stayed back and waited for movement in either of the rooms. When I didn't see any, I crouched down and jogged to the opposite side. My heart raced. If someone drove by, they'd see me. In the rush from the adrenaline coursing through my veins, I hadn't made either of us invisible to humans or magicals. If a human were to have seen us, they would have thought we were attempting to rob the house. Magicals would have thought worse.

I tiptoed through the bushes, praying to Goddess I wouldn't trip or step on a stick or something. I crouched down as low as I could and then took a few overdue breaths on the window's side. My senses went into overdrive. Every sound blasted into my ears: leaves bustling, bugs scurrying to get out of the cold. Every echo of traffic nearby roared through my head, every breath Cooper and I took. I needed to stay calm. My nerves were so jarred they tingled throughout my body. Why was it such a big deal? It could turn out to be nothing. I kept telling myself that until I gained the courage to peek into the room.

Two shadows moved along the space. My jaw fell open. I dropped to the ground. "Oh, my Goddess! Oh, my Goddess," I whispered. My entire body stiffened to the point I thought I would crack. "Look again, Abby," I told myself. And I did.

Waylon had his back to the window, his arms flailing up and down. His posture and movements indicated anger. I didn't move, hoping to catch a word or two as his jaw showed me his mouth was clearly moving, but I couldn't hear him, and I didn't read lips. He must have put a bubble around his home with some form of protective spell that didn't include magicals sneaking up to his windows.

When he moved to the side, I saw the person behind him look right at me.

Kaedan.

∼

I WHIPPED up a double protection spell over my apartment, then added another one for both me and Cooper. I chewed another nail until my finger bled as I paced my small living area. "He saw me, Cooper. What're we going to do?"

Cooper sat on the back of the couch scratching his belly. "First, you're going to calm down. Just because he looked out the window doesn't mean he saw you. And second, you're going to get me some rash cream. That ninja outfit did a number on my tummy."

"Oh, sorry." I held out my hand and a small tube of cream appeared. I walked it to Cooper. "Here."

He stared at me. "What am I supposed to do with it?" He stood on his hind legs and waved little front paws at me. "I don't have opposable thumbs."

"Right," I said. "Lie on your back, please." I opened the tube, squirted too much onto my fingers, and rubbed it on his belly.

He rolled over laughing.

"Cooper, stop. I haven't even rubbed it in."

"I can't help it. It tickles."

I groaned and attempted to massage it into his little red belly. He giggled and rolled onto his stomach. "I can't! I can't!"

"Come on. The last thing I need is Kaedan to show up here while I'm distracted."

He rolled back over. As I began rubbing the cream in, he laughed and rolled over again.

"Seriously?"

"It's cold, and it tickles," he said through short breaths. "Trust me. I'm not feeling good about this. It's embarrassing."

"I didn't know you were so ticklish." I scooped him up into my free arm, rested him against my chest, and held his front legs with that arm while I rubbed the cream on his inflamed belly.

He laughed, but only for a moment. "Oh, wow. That feels like a cool breeze on a hot summer day."

"Diaper rash cream is good for a lot of things."

He jerked his paws from my grip, rolled over in my arm, and dove onto the couch. "You put baby behind cream on my tummy?

"It's for rashes. Adults use it too."

His mouth opened, but only a sigh came out. "It does feel better."

"Good. Now can we figure out what to do next?"

The wind echoed outside and whistled as it hit the window. I crept over, pulled back the curtain and peeked outside. Nothing. The window rattled as the wind picked up and pushed into the old building. I opened it a crack just to stop the rattle and tasted the night air. Fresh and new, it reminded me of the first drink of water on a hot day.

Cooper scurried over and rubbed against my legs. "You should keep that closed. Just in case."

He was right. I pushed it down, and the fresh air was replaced by the stale, dry air hovering throughout my small apartment. I shuffled to the couch, grabbed my mother's throw from the other side, and wrapped it around me. I plopped down and groaned. "You might as well get some sleep. I'll stay up and wait for Kaedan."

Cooper nuzzled onto my lap. "No sleep for me. It's my job to keep you safe, and that's what I'm going to do."

Minutes later, his silky brick of a body vibrated with each snore.

17

I'd fallen asleep as well. Kaedan hadn't shown up, but I couldn't decide if that was good or bad news. It was possible he hadn't seen me. The room was dimly lit, it was dark outside, and I'd been dressed in black. Even if he had seen me, would he have known it was me? That ski mask hid my face. Maybe he'd seen someone, but didn't know who? If he did, and he thought it was me, wouldn't he have shown up at my place? I decided it was best to keep with my plan and act as though I hadn't been busted peeping into Waylon's home. If either of them acted differently toward me, I'd deal with it. Somehow.

Cooper and I finished our morning routine and headed down to the Enchanted. The aroma of freshly roasted coffee greeted us before we opened the door. Inside, the regulars, including Mr. Calloway and Waylon, sat by the fireplace reading newspapers, talking, and drinking their coffee. Sitting on the small tables framing the tiny space were books of every genre imaginable. Bessie must have been reorganizing or flushing out the ones she no longer wanted. Normally, the books were tucked away in their shelves.

The shop itself was small and cozy, the round tables and chairs crowding the space even more than the book section, which Bessie had always kept tidy. Messy or clean, it was my second home. It gave me peace, and I wouldn't have traded it for the world. The teenage girls from the other day sat at my table, talking and laughing, small books open amongst them. I set my things down a few tables away, giving myself space from their chatter so I could focus.

My editor would lecture me if I turned the first draft in late, but just like before, I couldn't focus on the story. There was just too much in my brain.

Bessie brought me a cup of coffee. "You look tired. How're you feeling this morning?"

"Tired, but I've got a deadline I can't miss, or I can't miss by much."

I opened my laptop and turned it on. Cooper climbed on top of the keyboard and moaned for food. "I'm starving."

"I've got you," Bessie said. "Let's go."

Cooper followed her to the kitchen. I watched Waylon engaging with his friends, wondering how he could act so nonchalant and carefree. I didn't like him, and I despised him latching onto Bessie the way he had. Whether he was somehow responsible for or involved with what was going on didn't matter. I'd lost any feelings of kindness toward the magical.

Bessie walked back out and stood beside me. We both stared at Waylon. "Don't worry," she said. "I'll take care of things."

"Bessie, I don't want—"

The door opened, and Remmington strutted in, wearing his full uniform. He sauntered over, ran his hand over the top of my head, and laced his fingers through my hair. I had to force myself from pulling away. "Hey you two, how's your morning?" He removed a toothpick in a plastic wrapper from his pocket, opened it, and stuck it into his mouth, leaving half of it sticking out of the corner.

"Just dandy," Bessie said. "Let me get you a coffee. Your regular?"

He smiled and nodded. "Thank you."

She scooted off. He sat down across from me. "Did you get any rest last night?"

"I did." My stomach flipped. I hated knowing what I knew, but I couldn't say anything without making things worse, so I played the part of a woman smitten with a man. "How about you?"

"Enough," he said. He studied me closely, his eyes narrowed and staring straight into mine. "You okay?"

I forced a smile. "Absolutely. I've come to a decision. I'm moving on from trying to find Gabe or the mountain man. Gabe is a powerful magical. He knows what he's doing. When he succeeds, he'll return. If I continue to stick my nose into this, it could make things worse for him. I don't want to do that." None of that was the truth, but if Remmington was involved, I needed him to think it was.

"Well, I can't lie. That's a relief. I've been trying to convince you of that for a while now. You're right. Gabe is a powerful magical. But Abby, if he does return, and I suspect that he will, what does that mean for us?"

Hadn't we already discussed that? Was he testing me? Testing my loyalty to him? If I said I'd pick Gabe, that would make things worse, but I'd told him before, I couldn't make any promises. So, what was I supposed to do? Suddenly change my mind? Maybe that was best. Maybe let him think I'd chosen him. I swallowed back the bile rising in my throat. "Gabe is my past. You are my present. I thought differently before, but I see how committed you are to us.

You would never do anything to hurt me, and I love that about you."

He blinked. "Really?"

I nodded, then took his hand in mine. "Remmington, Gabe's life is with the MBI. I understand that now. I lied to you. I didn't sleep much last night. I was up thinking about everything, and I realized I need a partner who's here for me. Someone to share my life with, not someone who's going to run off and put himself in long-term dangerous situations for a … a job." I squeezed his hand again. "It's like a lightbulb went off over my head. I see things clearly now."

Bessie returned with his coffee, but it was in a to-go cup. He narrowed his eyes at it as she handed it to him. "A to-go cup?" he asked.

"Absolutely," she said. "You're the chief of police, and you've got a job to do. We don't want to keep you from doing it."

"I always have a job to do."

"Well, I know that," she said. "But you're not always dressed in your uniform like you are today. I might not know a lot about policing, but I know something important is happening when the chief is dressed in his uniform."

"She's got a point, but I will say you look really nice in it."

His chest puffed out. "I do?"

"Yes," I said.

"Abby's always had a soft spot for a man in uniform," Bessie said. "You should have seen the crush she had on the mailman when she was a kid. She picked flowers for him from her mother's garden. Goddess, the yelling that ensued from that. Those flowers were important to her mother."

I didn't recall having a crush on the mailman, but I didn't say that.

"I do have something important happening today, so I should get going." He stood. "I'll call you later."

"You better," I said.

He walked toward the front door, smiled at Waylon and his friends, then headed out. I breathed for what felt like the first time since he'd walked in.

Bessie placed her hand on my shoulder. "Time to play the part." She walked over to Waylon and sat on his chair's arm.

Mr. Charming flew over, perched on Waylon's opposite shoulder, and said, "Bessie's the bomb! Bessie's the bomb!"

Suddenly, the kitchen door burst open, and a flash of a brown blob darted out and raced toward my table. It was Cooper, of course. He stuck his front paws out and screamed, "Coming in hot," before skidding into my legs.

I bent down and watched as he shook off the effects of the collision. "What's the rush?" I picked him up and sat him beside my laptop.

The girls a few tables away giggled.

"There's—" he said breathless. "There's a wolf spider in the kitchen."

I chucked. "A spider? Seriously? You're a cat, and you're a hot mess because of a spider?"

His little eyes widened. "It's a wolf spider, and she's got babies all over her back!"

I shook my head. "It's a spider. You're supposed to swat it and play with it, not run from it."

He climbed onto the table and spread his brick-like body over my laptop's keyboard. "Didn't you hear me? It had babies all over its back!" His breaths were short and shallow. "Thousands and thousands of babies!"

"Coop, take a deep breath. You're going to hyperventilate."

He breathed in and then blew out the breath, spreading the smell of tuna around me. "Okay. I'm better, but trust me, if I would have swatted it, those little terrors would have spread everywhere." He shuddered. "That's the stuff of nightmares, Ab."

I flicked my wrist and sent the wolf spider momma and her babies to a safe, comfortable, cat-free place. "You can stop shivering now. She's gone, and so are her babies."

He let out an exaggerated breath. "Thank Goddess. That thing was the size of my head."

"Good thing your head is dinky."

"Rude."

"Not rude. True."

Bessie's giggle stopped me short. "Oh, Waylon," she said as she wrapped her arm around his shoulders. "You're such a joker."

"That's not the word I'd choose," Cooper said.

"Right there with you."

18

I whispered close to Cooper's face. "Go over and listen to what they're saying."

He jerked his head back, and a double-furred chin appeared. It was cute. "Familiars don't snoop. We protect."

"Snooping is part of protecting. If we know what they're talking about, we may be able to plan instead of reacting."

"Plan what?"

I sighed. "We won't know unless you go snoop!"

"All right already, but I'm doing this under duress. Snooping is so catty."

"Well, you're a cat, so..."

He rolled his brown eyes. "That was weak."

I grinned as he sneaked stealthily on his itty-bitty toe pads around the back of the front counter, then behind Waylon's chair. He flattened himself as much as possible and crawled under it. It was a tight fit. Mr. Charming had bopped from chair to chair, but he must have seen Cooper hide because he dropped off one and wobbled on the floor toward Waylon.

"Coopie doopie do! Coopie doopie do!"

"Yes, Mr. Charming," Bessie said. "Cooper is here. We love him just as much as you."

"Coopie doopie do!" He bent his head down and stared under the chair. "Mr. Charming loves Coopie doopie do!"

Well, shoot.

Cooper crawled out from under the chair and batted at something I couldn't see. "Oh! I think I got it," he said.

Bessie smiled down at him. I caught her wink too.

Cooper sauntered back over in defeat. "Darn bird's got a big beak."

"That was inconvenient," I said.

"Yes, it was, and I had to pretend to swat a bug." He shook his head. "I've stooped lower than I ever thought I could."

"Oh, geez. Drama much?"

The front entrance opened. The girls nearby gasped when Kaedan walked in. At least I thought it was Kaedan in disguise. His normal, admittedly, nice-looking features had been replaced by a look almost identical to Chris Hemsworth.

Cooper hollered. "Thor's in the house!"

"Shh," I said. "It's probably Kaedan."

Bessie rushed to the counter and hollered toward the man. "Good morning, what can I get you today?"

He dropped his eyes toward Waylon as he walked by, but if you weren't looking, you wouldn't have noticed, because he didn't move his head. "Just a coffee," he said.

I immediately recognized the voice. Deep and soft with a hint of something that made it slightly different, but I'd have put money on it being Remmington, not Kaedan. His voice was deep as well, but it had a raspy edge to it.

"Did you see that?" Cooper asked. "The look between Waylon and that guy? Is that Kaedan?"

"I think it's Remmington," I said.

"Remmington? Let me check."

I stopped him from getting closer. "No. We can't let on. And just to be safe, keep it down."

"Why are we keeping it down?"

"Because I'm worried Kaedan lied, and he can actually understand you."

"Why do you think that?"

"I don't trust anyone right now. Most anyone, I mean."

"Right. So, change my language to something he won't understand."

"Like what?" I asked.

"I don't know. Something you'll understand but no one else will. Come on, hurry."

I flung my wrist. "Better?"

When Cooper spoke, I heard English, but his words came out in a tangled mess. He shook his head. "Seriously? That's what you came up with?"

"It's the best I can do."

"Fine. They've planned something."

"Whatever they're up to, I promise you it's no good," I said.

"You'd think Mr. Charming there would stop focusing on being annoying and start paying attention to the threats surrounding his charge."

"I'm sure he's paying attention. I think his technique is just different than yours."

"Inferior is more like it," he said.

Bessie handed the man his coffee. He paid her with a five-dollar bill. "Keep the change." As he turned around, he could have made eye contact with me, but instead, he just walked back to the door and left.

I crossed my arms over my chest. "What was that about?"

"He's watching you, Ab. Whoever it is."

My eyes widened so much they pulled the skin on my cheeks tight. I quickly placed another protective spell over us and dropped one over Bessie again just in case. If that was Kaedan wanting to hurt me, he was going to have to work hard to make it happen. My cell phone rang. The caller ID showed Remmington's phone number. "Interesting."

I answered the call, but before I could say anything, Remmington said, "That was me."

"In a Chris Hemsworth disguise? What's going on?"

"I'll tell you. Just meet me outside."

"Why?"

"I have information on Gabe."

I glanced at Cooper.

"What's he saying?" he asked.

"Why can't you just come in again?" I asked.

"Just come outside."

I disconnected the call, grabbed my things, and stuffed them into my bag, frustrated I hadn't gotten any work done, though I hadn't really expected to. "Let's go."

Bessie had walked back and sat on Waylon's arm rest again. "Where you off to so soon?"

"Duty calls," was the best answer I could come up with.

She raised her eyebrows. I just widened my eyes and walked out.

Remmington nor his version of Hemsworth were anywhere to be seen. I did a complete turn on my heels, checked down each direction on both sides, then across the street, but he wasn't there. Where could he have gone? "Remmington?"

Nothing.

Cooper's nose tilted up. He sniffed the air. "I don't like this. We need to get out of here."

"No. I want to know what's going on. Now." I took a few steps toward the direction Cooper had sniffed.

"Ab, stop! It's a trap!" A humongous black dog appeared from around the corner and charged toward us. Cooper hissed and raced toward it.

"Cooper, no!" The last thing I remembered was seeing the dog leap toward me.

19

My head hurt. I opened my eyes and closed them again. Everything was spinning.

"Abby? Abby, it's Bessie. Can you hear me?"

I groaned. "My head hurts." I tried to move my arm, but it was limp and heavy, and it took too much energy.

"No, don't move," Bessie said. "The ambulance is on the way. I can hear the sirens."

I was able to mutter, "Where's Cooper?"

"The ambulance just pulled up," she said, ignoring my question.

"Bessie, where's Cooper?" My head pounded. I finally gathered the strength to move my arm. I lifted my head a bit and touched the back of my head, feeling the blood matting my hair. "It was a dog," I said, and then the world went dark again.

I OPENED my eyes and closed them right away. The light was so bright it hurt to see it. My head pounded. I felt like I was going to be sick, and I was unbelievably tired.

"Abby?"

I squinted, letting one eye open to see who was talking to me. Remmington stood above me, looming over me like a monster. The ground had softened, and someone had put a sheet over me, but I didn't remember the sun shining that bright earlier. "Where's Cooper?" My words came out in a soft whisper, feeling like sandpaper against my sore throat. The light was too bright for me to keep even one eye open.

"I'm over here," Cooper said.

I tried to turn my head, but the movement caused a sharp pain to shoot through my brain. "Are you okay?"

"I'm fine, Ab. It's you we're all worried about."

I opened my eye again. "Why is the sun so bright?" I tried to speak louder, but my throat wouldn't have it.

"The sun?" Remmington said. His voice echoed in my ear.

"Shh," I said. "I have a horrible headache." A weight pressed against my chest, and then Cooper's face appeared centimeters from mine.

"I couldn't catch him, Ab. He was too fast."

It all came back to me. Chris Hemsworth. Remmington calling and saying that was him in disguise. Asking me to meet him outside. The monster-sized dog, and Cooper running toward it. I opened both eyes then, suffering through the bright light long enough to let them adjust. It wasn't the sun. It was lights, and I wasn't on the ground. "Where am I?"

Remmington touched my face. I turned away. My stomach churned. Had he attacked me? Had he sent the monster-sized dog for me? "Abby, it's me. We're at the hospital," he said. "You have a concussion. The doctors want to keep you overnight for observation."

"I've got to go." I attempted to sit up, but Cooper dug his nails into my gown. Their sharp points threatened to cut through my skin. "Nope," he said. "Just stay where you are."

I sighed. "Was it him?" I asked Cooper.

He flicked his head slightly toward Remmington. I wasn't sure what that meant.

"Did you see him?"

"We're pretty sure it wasn't a werewolf," Remmington said. "But we're not sure if it was a shifter or a real dog. I've got my people out searching, but we've not had any luck."

"It wasn't a shifter," I said.

"Abby, no more talking," Cooper said. "Tell your friend here he needs to leave because you're tired. We can talk when he's gone."

"Remmington, I'm tired. I want to rest. Can you come back later this morning?"

"It's after eight p.m., but I'll come back in the morning and see if I can take you home. How's that sound?"

It was night? How had that happened? Where had the time gone? I would wait until Cooper and I were alone to find out. "Good," I said, though I didn't think that.

He kissed my forehead. "I'm going to find whoever did this to you, and I'm going to make sure they never hurt anyone again. I promise you that."

"Thank you," I said.

He left then.

"Geez," Cooper said. "I didn't think he'd ever leave."

"How long have I been here?"

"All day. You've been sleeping on and off, but mostly on."

"Are you sure you're all right?"

"I'm sure," he said. "Abby, I don't think it was Remmington who barreled into you."

"How do you know?"

"It doesn't feel right. His smell has been weird for days. One day he smells normal, and the next. He's all funky smelling."

"It's probably just you. You've had so much tuna lately, Coop, and it's got such a strong smell. I'm sure everything smells weird."

"No," he said. "It's not that. I really don't think it's Remmington who tried to hurt you."

I exhaled, and a machine next to me beeped. "Then who was it?"

"I think it was Kaedan."

∽

I HIT the button on the side of the bed, and a nurse came in.

"Hello there, Ms. Odell. How are you feeling tonight?"

"Thirsty. Very thirsty."

"I expected that." She did something on the side of my bed, and it raised me into a sitting position. "Here you go," she said, handing me a large water bottle. "It's chilled to perfection." She raised her hand and held her palm toward the ceiling. A small plate appeared, and the scent of tuna invaded my nostrils. It made my stomach flip.

"Ick, that's not for me, is it?"

She giggled as she set it on the small table attached to the bed. "It's for your cat. I'm assuming he's your familiar?"

Cooper hopped onto the table. "I think I love this nurse." He stuck his face into the tuna and made obscene sounds as he ate.

The nurse watched him with wide eyes. "Does he always make those sounds when he eats?"

"You should hear him when it's mahi mahi. I don't feed it to him often for that reason."

She laughed. "Well, if you need anything else, just hit the button again. This is a no magic zone for our patients. You've got a big bump on the back of your head, and a grade one concussion. Goddess only knows what that's done to your magic. Resting and relaxing are all you're allowed to do tonight. You got that?"

I forced a smile, but the tuna smell made it hard. "Yes, ma'am."

∼

I WOKE up to a dimly lit room and Kaedan staring down at me.

I flinched and sent my head into a throbbing fit. Cooper had nuzzled himself in the crook of my neck. My flinch moved him, but he didn't move away. "What do you want?"

"Are you okay?"

Cooper's theory. The phone call asking to talk to me outside, the monster-sized dog attacking me. I needed to ask. "Did you set me up? Did you tell someone to attack me or was it you in one of your disguises?"

He blinked. "What? No. No, of course not."

"Then why did you lure me outside? Why not just talk to me in the Enchanted?"

"Abby, it wasn't me. I don't know what happened, but it wasn't me."

"Why should I believe you when just this morning you came into the Enchanted looking like Thor, acting like I wasn't even there. Then you left, and called me, and told me to go outside. Admit it, Kaedan. You set me up."

Cooper wiggled out of the small space and moved to the table. He glared over at Kaedan, hissing to make a point.

"I swear to Goddess, Abby. I wasn't at the Enchanted this morning, and I sure as heck wasn't disguised as Thor." He rubbed his chin. "Though that's not a bad idea."

"I don't believe you. Stop lying to me." I winced. My head pounded.

"Ab, relax," Cooper said.

I didn't, and I didn't care about relaxing. I cared about the truth. "What are you planning with Waylon? How is he involved in Gabe's disappearance and with the mountain man? What have you done to Gabe?"

His head dropped toward his left shoulder. "What? I don't know what you're talking about. It's got to be the medication. I'll tell you what. I'll come by your house once you're home. We can talk then. How's that sound?"

"No! I want to talk now."

But it was too late. Kaedan had disappeared in a cloud of dust.

I stared at Cooper. "I don't know what's going on."

"Neither do I, Abs. Neither do I."

"Do you still think it's Kaedan who sent that dog after me?"

"I'm not sure what to think anymore. None of this makes sense. My senses are all off. I don't know what's going on."

∽

THEY MUST HAVE GIVEN me something for pain because I had the strangest dreams that night. I dreamed of my mother skipping across a poppy field, and everything behind her turned to lavender. I dreamed about Gabe laughing and smiling and telling me things I couldn't understand. His mouth moved, but I couldn't make out the words. A man dressed in a pair of black pants and a grey button-down shirt slapped Gabe on the shoulder and pulled him into a hug. They patted each other's backs.

The monster-sized dog that had attacked me bounced over and rubbed his head up and down Gabe's side. Cooper jumped on his back and screamed, "Ride 'em cowboy!"

That was probably the least weird part of the dream.

Gabe and the man talked, but again, I couldn't make out a word they said. When the scene spun into a funnel and stopped, a new dream began. Or at least I thought it was a new dream.

Remmington and Waylon stood in front of a big, dark desk, their heads down and their hands behind their backs. Why were their hands like that? I couldn't see what was on top of or behind the desk. It took up too much space in my head, but I was able to rotate the visual in my mind to see their hands cuffed behind them. Why were they under arrest in my dream? Was it just a dream or a premonition? Whatever it was had made me shudder, and that's when I woke up.

Cooper stood staring at me on the table attached to the bed. "You okay?"

"This is bad, Cooper. It's really bad."

20

Three days passed, and though I was home, I wasn't allowed to do anything. Bessie and Stella made sure of that. It was absolutely awful. I was exhausted, and my head throbbed so much at times, I couldn't think straight.

Both women stuck close to my side, Bessie swearing she'd bind my powers if I tried any trickery. I wasn't sure she could, but I also didn't want to take any chances. Besides, I had a whopper of a headache still, and I needed the time to get well and make another plan.

Neither let Kaedan or Remmington in, and if they'd tried to get in on their own, Bessie must have put up a strong protective bubble to stop them.

The more I thought about it, the more I realized it had to be Remmington. I was sure of it. He'd done something to Gabe to get his job, and he'd somehow brought Gabe's brother Dexius into the mix. I didn't know who had the idea to allow Dexius to pose as the creepy mountain man with the clown nose, and I didn't care. If that was even Dexius and not Remmington posing as him. If it was Dexius, I'd make sure he never wore that thing again. I believed Remmington had sent the monster dog after me as a warning, what I couldn't figure out was why he'd disguised himself as a Thor lookalike.

Did he want me to back off my search? Did he think I was getting close? I considered telling Kaeden what I thought but decided against it. I didn't think I could trust anyone but Bessie and Cooper.

I finally had a plan, or another plan because I'd already had more plans than I cared to count, but I knew the newest plan would work. Not only would it lead me to Gabe, but to his brother Dexius.

First, I had to talk with Waylon again, tell him what I knew, and get him to tell me the truth. I didn't think he'd done anything to Gabe, but I had to be sure. My characters had never gone through anything similar, and things were well above my skill set, but my main characters always got their guy in the end, and I knew I would too.

I hated using magic on Stella, especially since she'd been amazing while I recovered, but I needed to get moving before it was too late. I'd wasted enough time and couldn't afford to waste any more.

Cooper stared at his twin staring back at him. "Uh, Ab?"

I chuckled at the look of shock and confusion plastered on his face.

"Did you seriously just clone us?"

I shrugged as my clone stepped into the room. "It's the best I could do without altering Stella in any way."

"Bessie isn't going to fall for this."

"Yeah, well, she doesn't have to. I've already cast a hiding spell on us, so if she does try to find us, she won't be able to."

He swatted at his clone who quickly swatted back at

him. "I don't like any of this," he said. "How do you even know which one is me?"

"Isn't it obvious? You haven't stopped complaining since you saw Cooper 2.0." I swapped my gnomes in tuxedos pajamas, the ones Bessie had bought me for Christmas the year before, for a pair of jeans, a long-sleeve black shirt, and a pullover black sweater. I slipped on a pair of black hiking books over my warm socks, added a baseball cap to the mix, and then whipped my hand into a circle and changed both Cooper and me into strangers.

He examined himself in my full-length mirror. "A tabby?" He stared up at me. "You turned me into an orange tabby? Couldn't you have at least made me a dog?"

I tapped my finger against my chin. "That's actually not a bad idea." I twirled my wrist, and Cooper morphed into a large German Shepherd.

He barked, and it boomed through my apartment. "Wow, as long as I don't slobber all over myself, I might be able to get used to this."

"German Shepherds don't slobber," I said.

"They do when they see a tasty treat walking by."

"You won't get hurt," I said. "I promise." I opened my bedroom door just enough to see Stella and Abby 2.0 playing Uno. I'd protected them from hearing us, and they had no clue we were there. Except Cooper 2.0. He hissed at the door. Go figure.

"Okay," I said. "Let's go."

And there we went, off to save the world, sort of.

∼

WE APPEARED in the reception area of the Holiday Hills Police Department. I rang the bell at the front desk and waited with Cooper, who I'd named Magnum, by my side.

"Magnum? Huh. I like that," he said.

"Shh."

A short, round woman with an outdated, gray beehive hairstyle slid the glass window open. She was so short she barely saw over the counter. "May I help you?"

"Yes, Melissa Sanders for Chief Sterling, please."

She hopped on the chair and peered over the counter through the glass. "Is that your dog?"

"Yes, ma'am." She stared at the dog. "Does it bite?"

"Only when I tell him to, ma'am."

Cooper growled. The woman shut the glass. "I'll get the chief for you."

We waited for about five minutes before Remmington arrived. He smiled as he walked through the door. "Ms. Sanders, nice to meet you." He bent down toward Cooper, who promptly showed his teeth and growled. Remmington popped right back up. "Trained well, I see."

"All my dogs are, Chief Sterling." I'd decided to play the part of the officer applying for the K-9 unit Remmington had decided to bring on board. I didn't mind sending her into a holding zone while I found Gabe.

"Come on back," he said. "I'm glad you've decided to come on board. I've already got an investigation I'd like to discuss with you." He smiled a little too much.

I sat in front of his desk, Cooper by my side. Remmington took his seat behind the desk and smiled again as he checked me out. Chills ran down my back. Had he always been that icky, or was it just to women he found attractive?

Yuck.

"I've got a situation. Initially, I'd intended to coax a

powerful witch into finding someone for me through a little reverse psychology."

I kept my shoulders straight and my words short and sweet. "I don't understand."

He exhaled. "I told her I wanted her to stay out of something because I thought she'd lead me to where I wanted to go, but things have changed. She's getting too close to things. I need her stopped."

"That doesn't sound like a job for the K9 team, sir."

"The job is what I decide it is," he said.

His authoritative tone didn't impress me. "Yes, sir. May I see the file?"

"There is no file. This is a powerful magical, and I want her handled."

"Yes, sir. Who is the witch?"

"Abby Odell."

I swallowed. Cooper growled.

Remmington stared at my cat/dog. "Is he always this intense?"

"Only toward people he doesn't like." I watched Remmington's Adam's apple bob up and down. "Wasn't this Abby Odell the one attacked by some dog on steroids? I heard people talking about it at that coffee shop."

"Yes, that's her."

"Did you send the dog after her?"

"It was a warning, but I suspect it didn't work. It's time to remove her from town. Do you understand?"

"How exactly do you expect me to do that?"

He stared down at the dog and then back up at me.

"You want me to sic my dog on a magical?"

"Yes."

I swallowed and forced myself not to flinch, for my face not to turn red, not to let the blood racing through my veins give away my identity. I couldn't show any emotion. I couldn't even hint to the fact that I wasn't who I claimed, and that I'd just learned my so-called sort-of boyfriend didn't care whether I lived or died.

Cooper growled.

"Sir, don't you think—"

He glared at me. "Abby hangs out at the Enchanted, that coffee shop you mentioned earlier. Like you said, she's been hurt, but she's recovering. I should have let the dog do its job."

"Sir, you're a police officer telling me you want to kill a witch. Do you understand the problem that creates for me?"

"I'm paying you to do a job. If you can't do it, then I suggest you leave."

"I could report you."

His eyes turned red. "Do that, and you and your mutt will regret it."

Cooper growled again. Remmington stared at him and then back at me. "Am I clear?"

I swallowed. "Clear, sir."

"She lives above the store. She goes in every morning, so get there and wait for her. Pets are allowed inside, but the owner is strict about it. If that mutt is mean, she'll kick you out."

"Magnum won't be mean, sir."

He stood. "Good." He gave me another once-over after I stood. "Report back to me tonight. I'll be having dinner at the Chinese restaurant just north of the Enchanted after six. I'll buy."

"Yes, sir."

Cooper and I stood outside staring up at Remmington's office window. "Now what?" he asked.

"We're going to stop Remmington, that's what."

21

Our clones only lasted a few hours before they ran out of juice. We rushed back to the Enchanted and disappeared up the back stairs. Once at my apartment door, I turned us back into our original selves and sent the clones packing.

Stella sat curled up next to me on the couch. Cooper was happy to get a can of tuna with only a bite or two missing.

"Stell," I whispered. She'd fallen asleep at some point. She must have been exhausted from being with me all night. I felt bad. "Stell, wake up."

Her eyes fluttered open. "Oh," she said, wiping a spot of dribble from her mouth. "Sorry. Can I get you something?"

"Yes. You can get me a rested best friend who stays at her own place from now on."

She yawned. "I don't know why I'm so tired."

"Babysitting is hard. Go home. I'm much better this morning." I glanced at my watch. "Or late morning. The doctor said I could get back to most of my regular activities today, and I'm ready. So, don't take this wrong, but get out of my apartment, now."

"Your wish is my command." She grabbed her things and tossed them into her bag. "I don't mean to offend you, but your couch stinks. I don't know how you can sleep on that thing."

"It's a gift."

I got to work after Stella left. I called the previous department Remmington had worked for, pretended I was with the mayor's office in Holiday Hills, and asked questions about his relationships and work ethic. Normally, those questions wouldn't be answered, but a little magic did the trick.

"Officer Sterling had his finer points," the head of the city's human resources department said. "But overall, he just wasn't a good fit. I understand he's the chief of police in your town now." The man laughed. "Can't say that didn't surprise me."

"Do you think he's qualified?"

"Are you asking because you're having issues?"

"We're concerned we rushed the decision," I said.

"If you're looking for a corrupt department, Sterling's your man. Now, I hate to rush, but I have a meeting to get to."

"Thank you for your time."

The next call I made was to the MBI. That one was especially tricky. I had to create a new cell phone account for Matilda Revere, a woman hired as a Holiday Hills human resources consultant a few years back. The call was a risk, but it was my only option. "Yes, I'm calling regarding a warlock named Remmington Sterling. He's currently the chief of police in Holiday Hills, Georgia."

The receptionist said, "Hold please."

A man picked up the line. "What do you need?"

Thank you for the kind greeting, I thought. "Information on Remmington Sterling. He's the—"

"Yeah, I know him. New chief in Holiday Hills. Replaced the old guy. What's his name? The guy that replaced Gabe Reynolds. Now that was a good warlock. Your Sterling? I wouldn't trust him with my ex-wife, and I can't stand the witch."

"Has he worked with the MBI before?"

"Sure has, but he's no longer affiliated with us. In fact, he's blacklisted. If he tries to get involved with any of our investigations, he'll regret it. We'd rather see that warlock dead than messing with our agents."

"Are you aware of any issues between him and Agent Reynolds?"

"Depends on what you mean by issues." He coughed. "Who are you again?"

"I'm with the human resources department for the city of Holiday Hills. We're reevaluating our employee roster."

"Fire the warlock," he said, and hung up on me.

Well. Remmington wasn't at all what I'd expected. He was worse.

22

A few hours later, it finally felt like I was getting somewhere. I had contacted the MBI again, under a different name and using a different cell phone number, requesting information about Kaedan. I didn't get anything other than he was an excellent agent. The firewall blocking magicals from accessing information from the MBI was thick, but I'd spent the rest of the day chipping away at it with spell after spell, hoping to break through and find something.

Cooper and I tossed around scenarios where Kaedan, then Waylon, was the bad guy, but some of the motives didn't match the crime. It had to be Remmington. He checked all the boxes.

But how could I be sure? What would my main character do? She'd go back to point A and start over.

I cast a spell to bring Waylon to me. He appeared in my apartment. "Abby?" He glanced around the small space. "Why am I here? Are you okay?"

"What happened with you and Gabe?"

He blinked. "What do you mean?"

"You said you wanted him out of Holiday Hills. Why?"

"Abby, you've been hurt. I think you need to get some rest." He turned toward the door.

"Waylon, I want the truth."

He flipped back toward me. "The truth is, I'm in love with Bessie, and I'm going to ask her to marry me. Do you think I'd do anything that would make her say no?" He shook his head. "I am a changed man because of Bessie. I'd never do anything to hurt her."

"Why was Kaedan at your house the other night?"

"Were you spying on me?"

I blinked. "I'm worried about Bessie."

"As am I. And yes, Kaedan was at my house. I asked him to come. Bessie's so worried about you, she can't think straight. I wanted to know what was going on with your search, and I asked Kaedan to tell me."

"That's it?" I asked.

"No, it's not. I also wanted to ask him to convince you to stop looking. Not only for your sake, but for Bessie's. She's a wreck over this. She believes you're in danger."

"You should have come to me."

"Kaedan is a powerful warlock. More powerful than you can imagine."

I relaxed. "No. I can imagine. He can block magicals, including the MBI, from seeing him, and I'm pretty sure he can understand my familiar."

"Like I said, he's a powerful warlock. Did you know he can manipulate technology? He does to us what we do to humans."

"What do you mean?" I asked.

"He shows us one thing, but we see another."

"How do you know?"

"Because he told me. He's going to find Gabe, and he's

going to make sure the mountain man is handled. He believes he's been taken into custody, and he's worried they'll arrest Gabe for his attempted murder. His plan is to find Gabe, and once he learns the truth, fix things. Please, Abby. Let Kaedan handle this. For Bessie's sake."

"What about that Thor lookalike? You two shared a look at the Enchanted. Did you know that was Kaedan?"

"The Thor lookalike?" His eyes widened. "Oh, right." He angled his head to the side. "That was Kaedan?"

"Waylon, don't play games. I saw you two look at each other."

"Well, sure I looked at him. When a Greek God comes walking into my view, I'm going to stare. Did we share a look? Not that I can recall."

Maybe we'd seen something more than what had actually happened? "You know what? I believe you. I believe you love Bessie, and I believe you asked Kaedan to your place to help protect us. I just don't understand why you'd lie to me about your confrontation with Gabe."

"I don't know what you're talking about, and I don't have time to figure it out. I need to be close to Bessie." He disappeared.

"Woah," Cooper said. "That was intense. I knew he cared for Bessie, but I didn't realize it was that much."

"I don't know if he's telling the whole truth. Why wouldn't he tell me about his confrontation with Gabe?"

"Maybe he just wants to keep it to himself? Maybe he's embarrassed?"

"I don't know."

"Do you think it could be him still?"

"Not really, but I want to make sure he's not going to hurt Bessie."

"Doesn't sound like he is."

"I'm not done talking to him."

"I figured."

The constant spell casting exhausted me. My head hurt, so I closed my eyes to rest for just a moment. The next thing I knew, Cooper was on my chest breathing his tuna breath into my nose. "Ab. Wake up. We've got to be at the Chinese place."

I checked my watch and flew off the couch, sending Cooper sailing in the air. He landed on all fours on the other side of my small coffee table. "Oh, sorry!" I said as I swapped us out for our alternate identities. "Let's go." I transported us to the back side of the Chinese place, gathered myself, and calmed my nerves, then walked toward the side of the building.

"Oh boy," Cooper said. He growled.

The mountain man stood just at the front side of the building, peering at us with his beady eyes.

I stepped back and stopped. Cooper growled. "No," I said.

"Abby, let me. I've got the teeth of a warrior. You know what I could do to that thing?"

I appreciated Cooper's desire to help, but I needed the mountain man to find Gabe. My entire body shook.

"Abby Odell, don't you look different?" he said. He spun his hand over his head, and everything around us disappeared. Where were we? Were we still in Holiday Hills, or had he taken us somewhere else?

I begged my bravery to kick in, and when it didn't, I did what any witch would do. I faked it. "I've been looking for you. I know who you are. Where's Gabe? What have you done to him?" Sounding brave was hard when your teeth chattered.

"I'm here to warn you. Things are not as they appear," he

said. "Witchcraft is flooded with trickery. Watch yourself."

Was he for real? "I'm not afraid of you! You can't scare me with your senseless talk. Now take me to Gabe, or I'll... I'll—"

He laughed. "Turn me into a frog?" He laughed some more. "My powers are far greater than yours, but I'm not here to hurt you, Abby. I'm here to warn you. This is more dangerous than you think. Tread carefully."

"What's that supposed to mean?"

"You're missing the obvious. There are clues. Find them, and you'll find what you're looking for."

"I'm looking for Gabe, and I know you know where he is, so stop feeding me all this, I don't know what, and take me to him."

I'd had Cooper on a leash, but he broke free and charged the mountain man. Only an inch away, the man disappeared, and bam! Holiday Hills appeared again.

I bent at my waist and took a deep breath. He hadn't killed me, but he hadn't given me anything solid either. Or had he?

"Abby?" Cooper said. "He didn't smell right."

"What?"

"I've smelled the mountain man before, and this guy didn't smell like him. I don't think it was him. Now granted, my cat nose is a billion times better than this cold, wet schnoz, but it's still pretty darn good. Speaking of noses, did you see? He wasn't wearing the clown nose. I'd bet one of my nine lives that wasn't the real mountain man. It was Remmington disguised as him."

I pressed my lips together. "Or maybe it was the real one."

∼

"Abby Odell spent the day in her apartment," I said to Remmington. "There was a woman with her until shortly after I began my watch. She smelled like a human. No one else appeared."

"They could have gotten in without you seeing," he said. He used his chopsticks to eat a pot sticker.

"No," I lied. "I created a barrier no one could pass through. I sent Magnum out looking, but it was her in her apartment.

"Keep at it. I don't care what you have to do. I want her gone."

"I'll do what I can," I said. "I did spend some time at that bookstore, the Enchanted. I was surprised at how good the coffee was, by the way, but I learned a lot there. For example, I learned you and the witch you've hired me to handle, are dating. I can't help you if you're not telling me the truth."

He tapped his chopsticks on his plate. "Let's just say things aren't always as they seem."

"With all due respect, sir, if I don't understand the full scope of my assignment, I can't perform at my best. What is this goal, and why is there an MBI agent working with her to achieve it?"

"Disregard the MBI agent. He's harmless. I like Abby, but she is primarily a means to an end. Our relationship started so I could keep an eye on her. I even cast a spell, so she'd forget about Reynolds, but she wormed her way out of it. Now she's obsessed with finding him, and I can't deal with her much longer. My goal has changed, and that's what matters most."

"And that is?"

"To make sure Gabe Reynolds doesn't return to Holiday Hills. Permanently."

I pressed my lips together. "So, you're saying you want to eliminate both Abby Odell and Gabe Reynolds?"

"Because I want to keep my job. I wanted this job for a long time. I finally have it, and I'll do whatever it takes to keep it."

"Couldn't you have just eliminated Gabe Reynolds to get it before?"

"I thought about that," he said. "But decided it would be more fun to ruin his reputation and make him suffer the way I've suffered. The problem is, he was sent on a Magical Bureau mission, and he's gone MIA. I've done everything I can to find him, but he's disappeared into thin air. I need to figure out a way to make that disappearance last forever, and that's where you come in."

"And the witch?"

"An unfortunate problem that must be handled."

"Are you sure that's a good idea?" I asked. "Wouldn't that be risky considering your ultimate goal?"

"I'll do what needs to be done to reach that goal."

Cooper's dog version stood at the edge of the table. He looked at me, then shifted his head toward Remmington and sniffed the air. He sneezed. We made eye contact, and I just knew he wanted to tell me something. I exhaled as I stood. I needed to get out of there. I needed to wrap my head around what I'd heard. "I'll see what I can do."

"Don't see, just do it."

I nodded and walked out, then transported Cooper and I back to my house.

Cooper sat on the back of my couch. "Either Remmington's got some hormonal issues or something, or my nose is still out of whack."

"Did he smell funky again?"

"Yes."

"Maybe it's his laundry detergent or something?"

"It's something, for sure," Cooper said.

I sat on my couch in complete shock. Remmington had sucker punched me multiple times. First, he'd faked being kind, then he faked liking me, cast a spell to make me forget the man I loved, and that goal of his? That was the worst. He wanted to eliminate me and Gabe.

And I wasn't about to let that happen.

23

I requested Kaedan's presence. Surprisingly, he responded quickly, showing up standing in front of my coffee table. "How are you feeling?"

"Before I answer, may I ask you a question?"

"Of course."

"Why were you at Waylon's the other night?"

He blinked. "At Waylon's? You mean his house?"

"Yes."

"I wasn't. What makes you think I was?"

"I saw you there."

"No, Abby. You didn't see me because I wasn't there. I've never been to Waylon's house, and I've never had any association with him."

"I think I owe you an apology. For a while, I thought you were the one who attacked me, but I was wrong."

"Apology accepted. What's happened to change your mind?"

"Remmington and Gabe didn't get along. Gabe had suspended him prior to his mission, and somehow Remmington got the previous interim chief fired and took his place. He's told me he's the official chief, but the human officers said he's an interim. They think he's somehow manipulated the mayor. He's hired a K-9 specialist to handle me and eliminate Gabe. He said I'm a means to an end. I think he's been posing as the mountain man, and I think he's the one who attacked me."

He sat in the chair next to the couch. "That's a lot to take in."

"I know." I leaned forward. "I need you to help me trap him. I want him to lead me to Gabe."

He stared into my eyes. "Okay."

~

That time, I didn't come up with the plan. Kaedan did. Before we could execute it, I needed to talk to Bessie, Stella, and Remmington.

"You can't tell anyone, not even Waylon," I said to Bessie.

"But you don't think he's involved?"

"No, and I told him that." I grimaced. "Sort of. I was rude. I will have to apologize."

"No, you don't. I can do that. You have more important things on your plate right now," she said. "And don't worry about Stella. I'll handle things with her."

"Thank you," I said.

"Abby, please take care of yourself. I'm worried about this."

"I have Kaedan to help."

"And you think you can trust him?"

"I have to."

She exhaled. "That doesn't make me feel any better."

"It's the best I can do."

I left Bessie with a big hug and a promise I'd be in touch and headed straight to the police department.

Remmington saw me immediately. "Hey," he said. He kissed my cheek. "I'm surprised to see you up and about. How're you feeling?"

"Better, thanks. I'm sorry Bessie and Stella kept you away, but it did help me rest and heal, not seeing anyone."

"I understood. I'm just glad you're better." He hitched his backside up onto the corner of his desk. "Have you decided to give up the search?"

I looked down at the floor and then up at him. "Yes. Bessie and I had a long talk. I don't know who or what came after me, and we've both cast a dozen spells to try to find the truth with no luck. Bessie strongly suggested I let things lie, and I am. My life is worth more than anything I was trying to do."

"I'm glad. If you want me to continue looking, I can."

"No. I'm dropping it. I'm sorry if it's disrupted things between us. Are we okay?"

"We are great."

"Good, then I need you to know I'm going away for a bit. Not long, and not to search for Gabe or the mountain man."

He bent his head to the side. "Where are you going?"

"I'm so behind in my manuscript, if I don't focus on it, it won't be done, and I don't want to jeopardize my new publishing contract. This is my livelihood."

"Can't you just use magic?"

"No. That would be phoning it in, not to mention unethical, and I can't do that. My writing is important to me."

"Where are you going?"

"I haven't decided."

He hopped off the desk and crouched down in front of me. "Are you sure that's what's going on?"

"Yes," I said.

"Okay then. When you get back though, I hope I'm the first person you see."

"I promise you will be."

Kaedan was sitting on my couch when I returned. "How'd it go?"

"We're all set. Is that van of yours ready?"

"It is," he said.

"Then let's do this."

Cooper and I became cop and K-9 once again.

"Wow," Kaedan said. "That's a big difference. I wouldn't have guessed that."

"Really?" I asked. "You don't see me as a cop?"

"I'm talking about Cooper."

"I don't like this magical," Cooper said.

I laughed. "Wish me luck."

"Luck," he said.

∼

A CROWD GATHERED outside City Hall. I glimpsed the podium and wondered what was happening. The mayor walked out and stepped up to the podium. "Thank you for coming by," he said. "I can assure you we are doing everything we can to address the situation. Once I have more information, I'll schedule a news conference. Thank you." He nodded once, and his assistant rushed him back inside as the group hollered out questions.

I recognized the reporter standing near me. It was Jessie Rosenblatt from Channel Six News in Atlanta. I asked what was going on.

"Someone leaked that someone in the mayor's office has stolen a few hundred thousand in city dollars."

"Really? That's awful."

"Maybe, but it's fantastic news for a reporter. Especially in this strange little town."

"Lovely," I said. I headed into the station with Cooper as the dog by my side. "I'm here for Chief Sterling."

"Yes, ma'am," the receptionist said.

Remmington met us at the reception desk and walked us to his office. After closing the door, he said, "What do you have for me?"

"I've learned your witch is planning to leave."

"She's going to work on her novel."

"Are you sure?"

"She told me herself. She's assured me she's going to stop her search for Gabe Reynolds."

"I've learned otherwise."

He tilted his head to the side. "What are you saying?"

"I've learned she's pretending to leave for the book but has a lead on this Gabe and is off to find him."

"How do you know that?"

"I am a powerful witch, Chief Sterling."

He narrowed his eyes at me. "Your work here is done."

Cooper growled.

"Excuse me? I thought you—"

He held up a hand and stopped me from continuing. "Please. I'll be looking for another K-9 team. Thank you for your time. The receptionist will issue you a check on your way out."

"But—"

"If you don't mind, I'm leading an investigation into our corrupt government, and I must get on with it. Thank you for coming by."

I nodded once and walked out. Step one in our plan was a success. Remmington believed I lied to him. He would search for me, and if we were lucky, Gabe would find him first.

Ten minutes later, Remmington called my cell. "I'm going to be out of touch for a bit. Looks like someone inside our local government is stealing, and I'm leading the investigation. Are you going to be okay?"

"I'll be fine. I'm heading out to finish this book. I need to get away to do it."

"Are you sure that's a good idea?" Remmington asked.

"Why wouldn't it be?"

"I just worry about you."

"I appreciate that, but I'm a big witch. I'll be fine."

"I know you will."

After we disconnected, I said to Cooper. "He's just confirming if I'm leaving or not."

"Sounds about right."

∼

I MET Kaedan in his van. "Anything yet?"

I sat in a chair and calmed myself. "Let me check." I closed my eyes and focused on the energy surrounding me. The idea was to force Remmington into casting a location spell on me and rerouting it to Kentucky, where I would have gone to find Gabe. I breathed in and out, and then it happened. I saw the energy circle around me. It glowed a deep red. "He's done it! What do we do now?"

"We don't do anything. I'm going to Kentucky to bust Remmington and put him away forever."

"And that will bring Gabe back?"

"If Remmington is posing as the mountain man, then once I have Remmington, the MBI will force him to remove the morphing spell, and we'll be able to locate Dexius, which should lead us to Gabe."

"And if it doesn't?"

"It will, Abby. I'll be in touch." He disappeared.

Hours passed. I played checkers with Cooper, who beat me twice and knocked my confidence down in the checkers world. I paced the small van, waiting and hoping for Kaedan to return with Gabe, but it hadn't happened. "I can't take this much longer."

"I'm surprised it's taken this long," Cooper said. "Can you locate where you're supposed to be in Kentucky?"

"I don't need to. I've got a location spell on Kaedan. We can go right to him."

"I was afraid you'd say that, but I'm glad you did."

∼

"Wow," Cooper said.

"Shh, we don't want them to hear us."

Standing in that Kentucky forest felt like we'd stepped back in time. Mountains with rock formations protruding from their sides with moss and ivy growing on them shaded the area, but it wouldn't have mattered. The trees and wild plants growing freely were impossible to see through anyway. I half expected a Tyrannosaurus Rex to pop out from behind a rock. About ten feet from us was a small wooden shack with boarded windows and a rusted out pickup truck on the right side. "This is scary," I whispered. "What if Remmington's in the house?"

A bug hovered near my face. I raised my hand to swat at it, but realized it wasn't a bug. It was a fairy. "Be careful, witch. Things are not as they seem," she said.

I clenched my fists. "What does that mean? Can you please just tell me?"

She giggled. "The forest is full of danger." With that, she buzzed away.

"I don't like fairies," Cooper said.

"I'm beginning to feel the same."

Leaves rustled ahead. I dropped to the ground and peered through a small break in the trees.

"It's Kaedan," Cooper said.

That meant Remmington would show up any minute. I was sure of it.

24

"Why is he just standing there?" Cooper asked.

Kaedan surveyed the area, bent down, picked up a stick, studied it, then tossed it aside. He turned in a circle, slowly eyeing his surroundings. Had he heard me? Did he know we were there?

"I don't know. Where's Remmington? Shouldn't he be here looking for me? If he knows I'm searching for Gabe, he should be here too."

"I'm confused," Cooper said.

"Should I say something?" I whispered.

"No. You might scare him. He could hurt you without meaning to."

Kaedan wasn't the type to scare easily. He looked our direction.

"This is ridiculous," I said. "He's not doing anything anyway." I stood and moved through the small brush of trees and shrubs. Cooper followed. When I worked my way out of them and onto the partially cleared land where the house was located, I bumped right into Kaedan.

"Abby? What're you doing here? You're not supposed to be here."

"Well, I am. Is that where Gabe's hiding out?"

"Come inside. They can see you out here."

"Who's they? Is Remmington bringing someone? Is it the mountain man?" I asked trailing behind him as he jogged toward the shack. Cooper followed me in and immediately darted off toward what had to have been the kitchen.

He closed the door behind us. "He wouldn't come alone. Listen," he moved toward a cabinet in the back of the shack. "You really shouldn't be here. This is dangerous. I need you to stay safe."

"I'm not safe as long as Remmington is trying to hurt people I care about."

Cooper darted toward Kaedan. I watched Kaedan look down at him and grunt.

"He's just going to rub your legs. He likes to claim his friends," I said.

Cooper did just that, rubbed his face over Kaedan's leg. He stepped back and shook his little brown head, then ran back to me. I glanced down at him, but he kept his eyes focused on Kaedan. What had he smelled?

Whatever had Cooper nervous hadn't phased Kaiden. He turned toward the cabinet and removed a small box from its top drawer. I watched as a tiny plastic wrapper dropped to the ground. When he turned around, I saw the toothpick in his mouth. "Would you like one? They're cinnamon."

Cooper meowed.

A cinnamon toothpick? I swallowed. "No, I'm fine. Thanks."

"Abby," he said stepping closer. "You really need to go. Please."

I placed my hand on his bicep. It was firm and bulky. I stepped back. The cinnamon toothpicks. The change in muscle texture. Mr. Calloway not remembering being at the Enchanted. Waylon said Kaedan could manipulate things like we manipulated magic to humans. He was right. Kaedan had done it with me. The van. The dark web. All of that. It was all a trick.

A trick! Trickery, like the fairy said. Enemies can be friends.

Wow. How had I missed it all? It wasn't Remmington. He wasn't the bad guy. It was Kaedan. It had been Kaedan all along. He'd pretended to be Remmington. My mind raced through everything that had happened since Kaedan arrived.

Remmington didn't like cinnamon, but Kaedan didn't know that. My body tensed. I couldn't believe I'd fallen for his tricks. And why? Why would he go to such extremes? What did Gabe have on him?

I racked my brain trying to figure out what to do. I could have used magic, but anything I did could prevent me from finding Gabe, and Kaedan was a powerful warlock. He'd done so much already, and I had no idea what else he could do. My only option was to stay calm and play along. I needed to know the why, and then I could figure out what to do about it. "I can help you, Kaedan," I said. "I have to do this. Please let me."

He pressed his lips together and nodded. "Okay. Fine. You might as well stay. I'm going to need some assistance, and if you're here, maybe Gabe will come out of hiding to help us catch Remmington." He lifted his head toward the ceiling. "Gabe! I know you're close by, and I know you can hear me! Abby's here. Remmington's coming. Let's handle it together. Please. I can help you with the MBI."

He'd thought I was naïve and desperate. He thought I'd think something as simple as calling for Gabe would work? If so, he would have returned months ago. It was a lie. It had all been a lie. It had been a trap. He'd planned it all along. Get me to trust him, then manipulate me to help him so he could use me as a bargaining chip. Then, bam! Gabe shows up, and Kaedan gets rid of him forever. But why? Why did Kaedan want to get rid of Gabe?

My thoughts raced. I needed to figure it all out before things got worse. I needed a plan to stop Kaedan from finding Gabe. I'd rather Gabe be gone forever than let Kaedan do something terrible to him. I had so many questions. What about the mountain man? Where did he play into everything? Was he even Gabe's brother? Had he been a made-up character in a horrible thriller, or was he truly Gabe's brother? "What about the mountain man? Do you think he'll come?"

The wind blew through the cracks of the wood covering the windows. Something howled a deep, guttural howl, outside. My body shivered. Cooper sauntered over like nothing important had happened. Had he not heard a thing? He rubbed his face into Kaedan's leg again, but the warlock ignored it.

I was afraid to speak. Anything I said could have given me away. I couldn't have that. The wind picked up, howling as it beat against the shack. The wind blew the door open again. Kaedan strutted to it and slammed it shut. He looked out through a crack in the window and nodded. "He's close, and I don't think Gabe's coming, Abby. I'm sorry. I thought this would work. I thought we could bring Gabe here and that he could help us take down Remmington, but I was wrong." He walked back to the cabinet and took another toothpick from the box.

I picked Cooper up and whispered in his ear. "Go with me on this." I switched his language so Kaedan couldn't understand him.

"What's going on?"

I mouthed, "It's not Remmington. It's Kaedan." I knew he'd respond, so I switched his language to cat meows and gave myself the ability to understand them.

His little nostrils flared. "I knew he smelled wrong. He smelled like Remmington. No," he said shaking his head. "He smelled like Kaedan pretending to be Remmington. How did I miss that? And that cinnamon? It's so strong. I should have pushed you on it. I should have paid better attention to the smells."

"No, I whispered. "You weren't sure. It's okay."

"What's going on with you two?" Kaedan asked. My heart stopped beating. He studied Cooper. "Why is he meowing so much?"

Thank Goddess. My heart beat again. "I didn't feed him before we came. He's hungry." "Hey," I said to Kaedan. "May I have a toothpick?"

He turned around. "Sure."

He handed me one. Cooper jumped out of my arms. "That's too strong up close like that."

I twirled it in my hand and spoke as calm and casual as I could muster. "I've been thinking. I need to be honest with you."

He tipped his head to the side. "Okay."

"I saw you at Waylon's house the other night. Why were you there?"

"How did you see me?"

"I'm a witch. Do you really have to ask?"

"I was eliminating suspects. That's my job. I'd learned Waylon and Gabe had problems, and I wanted to find out what happened between them."

"Did you?"

"Abby, I don't think this is something we should be talking about."

"Why not?" I asked.

"Because I know you don't want to see Bessie get hurt."

"Then you should definitely tell me."

"Fine," he said. He stepped toward one of the boarded-up windows and looked outside.

"Gabe arrested Waylon for loitering. He'd been stalking a witch for some time apparently."

"Did Waylon say that was true?"

He shook his head. "Why would he admit to something like that when he knows how close we are?"

Lies. Everything he said were lies. "Gabe never mentioned you. Why is that?"

"Because he's the kind of warlock that keeps a lot of things to himself."

"I guess. Remmington's not like that."

"Remmington's not the warlock you thought he was. I'm sorry about that, Abby."

I rubbed the toothpick between my thumb and forefinger. "This is cinnamon."

"Yes."

"Did you know Remmington doesn't like cinnamon? It bothers his stomach."

Kaedan's lip curved into a snarl. "Well, that's unfortunate, isn't it?" He stepped closer.

"The vision is mine to see."

He took another step and laughed. "That only works when I want it to. You're seeing what I want you to see, little witch. I am too powerful for you."

"Oh yeah? We'll see about that." I backed up, and with

my finger pointed at Kaedan, I twirled it, and said, "Witches and warlocks, haters and lovers, show me the man undercover!"

Kaedan turned into the mountain man.

"Oh, boy," Cooper said. He pushed his way in front of me and stood as a protective block from Kaedan.

Kaedan stared down at him and laughed. "I don't want anything from you. I want Gabe. You're simply a means to an end." He took another step toward me. "But if I must, I will eliminate you forever."

"You're the mountain man?"

He sneered. "I am whomever I choose to be. I am the mountain man. I am Remmington. I am Mr. Calloway."

Cooper hissed. "I knew he smelled funky!"

Tears fell from my eyes. "Enemies can be friends."

"That was the closest I came to worrying you'd learn the truth. That little fairy bug needs to be squashed, but she'll have to wait her turn. It's Gabe I want. He deserves everything I've planned for him."

"What about me? You've been tormenting me for months. Did I deserve that? Why are you doing this? Are you Gabe's brother?"

He laughed. "You really don't get it, do you? Gabe isn't looking for his brother. He's looking for me. I'm Dexius K. Kredum, or to you for all these months, the mountain man. Now is the perfect opportunity for Gabe and me to meet again."

I bit back the anger from rising inside me. "Does Gabe even have a brother?"

He sneered. "You'll have to address that with him, if I give you that opportunity."

"I get it now. Gabe's mission was to find you. He hasn't gone rogue. You lied. You lied about everything. You pretended to help me because you thought it would lead Gabe back. You wrote that letter from him, didn't you?"

He laughed. "That was the one thing I didn't think to do. Imagine how upset I was to learn he'd made contact without returning. I didn't expect that from him."

"That's because he knows," I said. I wasn't sure if that was true, but I went with it. "He knows what you're doing, Kaedan, or is it Dexius? He's watching."

"Think again. Then why would he approve of Remmington?"

I didn't have an answer for that. "You're using me as a trap. You think Gabe will come for me."

He flipped the toothpick to the fresh side. "For a witch with such power, you're not very smart. I feel sorry for you, Abby. I really do. Like I told you when I impersonated Remmington. You're a means to an end."

I took another step back. There wasn't much space left between us. I had to act fast or risk Goddess only knew what. I squeezed my eyes shut and dug into my memory. Why? Why would Kaedan, or rather Dexius, be doing this? Why would Gabe be looking for him? I gasped. "This has to do with your partner, doesn't it? You're the one who killed her, and Gabe knows, doesn't he? You went to prison, and now what? You're out, and Gabe wants to stop you from killing any more witches?" I shook my head. "No, that's not it. He knew you'd come after him, so he went looking for you."

"Now you're catching on." He twisted his hand, and a ball of fire appeared in his palm.

Cooper hissed.

"The dark web. The MBI files. Those were all lies, weren't they?" I tried to stall him.

He spit out the toothpick and sneered

I squeezed my hands into fists and yelled "Tell me! Did you write that letter?"

A loud crack of thunder boomed outside. The shack shook. I loosened my fists as more tears spilled from my eyes. "Tell me!"

"I should have," he said.

"Your plan to kill me so he'll show up and you can kill him. It all makes sense now."

He snarled again. "I guess you're smarter than I thought."

I should have been smarter. He'd fooled me for too long. "Reverse psychology. You played me all along. Let me think you didn't want me involved in finding Gabe, then said you'd help because you thought I'd lead you to him." I threw my arms up in the air and laughed. "Well, how'd that work out for you?" I glared at him. "Gabe's not coming. He knows you've set a trap, and he knows I'm powerful enough to take you on." I twirled my hand, and a ball of fire appeared in it.

He took another step closer.

I held out the ball of fire. "Don't come any closer, or I'll send you away forever."

He snarled. "Abby, you poor little witch. You're still new at this. You have no idea who you're dealing with."

"Yeah? Well, neither do you." I flung the ball of fire at his chest, then shoved my fists toward him. Bolts of lightning lit up the small room as they smacked into his chest. He jerked back, but they didn't hurt him.

"That's it," he said with a laugh. He held his ball of fire up next to his ear. "Wear yourself out. Gabe will feel this. He'll feel your distress, and he'll come. I've waited years for this. That warlock will finally pay for what he did to me."

My blood boiled. I refused to let him use me so he could

kill Gabe. I prayed to Goddess for all the powers of past witches to fill my soul. I needed them. I needed to stop him.

Cooper hissed. His back end rose.

"Cooper, no!" I screamed.

It was too late. He propelled himself into the air, attaching his front claws onto Kaiden's cheeks. "Uh-oh," he yelled. His claws began sliding down Kaeden's gnarly beard. He latched onto the warlock's shoulders and dug in his claws hard enough for Kaedan to growl.

He grabbed Cooper, but before he had a chance to do anything, I whipped balls of fire at his feet. Over and over, the flames hit. He jumped back, dodging the heat and fire. Cooper fell and leaped over the flames. He ran back to me, stood in front of me, and screamed in that funky language for me to turn him back into the German Shepherd.

I did.

Kaedan's eyes widened. He took a step back and pitched fire at Cooper. Cooper whipped his head left and right, dodging the flames as his mouth swung drool from side to side. He growled that deep, guttural sound. I'd never heard a sound like that come out of Cooper as a cat. I knew he was showing Kaedan his teeth.

Kaedan flinched, but he quickly regrouped and drew his hand back. Multiple balls of fire swirled around his palm.

Cooper stepped forward.

"No," I screamed. I launched ball after ball of fire toward Kaedan, deflecting his flames from hitting Cooper. One caught his beard and set it on fire.

He yelled. His hands shot into the air above his head and swords appeared. Cooper lunged at him. The swords flew toward him.

I screamed. "Cooper!"

The front door burst open. "Abby!"

The swords twisted around in the air, ripped through Kaedan's shirt, and stuck him to the wall.

I leaned forward and held myself up with my hands on my knees. I could barely breathe. Cooper rubbed his dog face against my knee. "Ab, turn around."

I took a deep breath, and with all the strength I had, stood up and turned. Remmington, Gabe, and a man I didn't recognize rushed toward me. I backed away, unsure of how to react. I stared into Remmington's eyes, then I looked into Gabe's, and then the man I didn't know. "Who are you?"

He pivoted toward Gabe.

"This is my real brother, Abby. His name is Jim," Gabe said.

I stood there for a moment and laughed. "Jim?" I pointed to the man who looked a lot like Gabe. "Your name is Jim?" I laughed harder. "Jim," I said through it. I turned toward Cooper. "His name is Jim!"

25

"Well, that was a wild ride," Cooper said. I set a plate of salmon and tuna on my small dining table. He climbed up and looked at it. "You'd think I'd snarf this down in a heartbeat, but I'm not hungry." He shook his tiny cat head. "Wow. I've said that twice now, in the same life. Weird." He pushed the plate away with his little paw and pawed for me to hold him. "I'm worried about you. What're you going to do?"

That was the same question I'd asked myself over and over. Things had happened so fast, and even two days later, I still needed to process it all. A knock on my door stopped me from responding.

"It's Remmington. Don't answer it," Cooper said.

"How do you know?"

"My nose knows." He hung his head and sighed. "I should have paid attention to it earlier, but I didn't."

I exhaled. "No, I need the truth. I can't hide in my apartment forever." I opened the door. "Come in."

Remmington hesitated but walked in and stood by the table. He had a toothpick in his mouth. I closed the door.

"Is that cinnamon?" I asked.

He blinked. "No. I can't eat cinnamon. It gives me an upset stomach."

"Just making sure."

"Because?"

"Kaedan didn't know you didn't eat cinnamon."

"Oh. I'm so sorry. The interviews are complete. I understand what happened now."

"I'm glad someone does."

"Is that what made you realize Kaedan, or Dexius, was posing as me?"

"For the most part."

He pursed his lips, then smiled.

I sat on the couch. Cooper sat beside me.

"Abby, some of what you learned about me is true. I had problems at other departments. Gabe gave me a chance here, and I was glad. I'd changed. I'm a better warlock. Or, I was, but I blew it. The first time I saw you, I just... I just knew you were the one. And stupid me thought I could steal you away from Gabe."

I wiped the tears from my eyes. "Did you threaten him?"

He shook his head. "No. I might be dumb, but I'm not stupid. I know he's a powerful warlock. I just acted like a high school punk. He called me out on it. The day he left to find Dexius, he suspended me. When he left, I went to the interim chief and told him Gabe said he'd wanted to promote me, put me on the route to detective or something. He had no idea the mayor would fire the interim chief and put me in the position. I still don't know how that happened, but there's an investigation into some money issues, and I think someone's trying to make me the fall guy."

"Were you involved in it? In what happened?"

"No. I promise, but I did want to make sure Gabe didn't

come back. I knew you wanted to find him, and watching you suffer through that? That was heartbreaking for me. I couldn't stop you, and I knew that. But I had no idea Dexius was pretending to be me."

I believed him. "Okay."

"There's more. Gabe came to me about thirty minutes before we showed up at the shack. He said you were in trouble. He knew about us, but he didn't care. He said all that mattered was keeping you safe, and he was right. I apologized to him, and I owe you that apology as well. I started our relationship with dishonesty. I lied by omission, and I know that's wrong. I'm sorry."

"Thank you for being honest with me."

"You should know I'm leaving. I've taken a transfer to a department in Colorado. I think the distance will be good for me."

I wanted to hug him, but it didn't seem appropriate. "Thank you for being there for me. I did have feelings for you, Remmington, but—"

He held out his hand. "The better warlock won. Good luck, Abby, and please, stay safe." He turned toward the door and walked out.

Cooper climbed onto the couch. "Whoa. That was intense."

"I'm going to bed," I said.

"Sounds like a plan," Cooper said. I changed into my pajamas and snuggled under my covers with Cooper's warm body rolled in a tiny ball next to me.

∽

THE NEXT MORNING, I showered and prepared for the day as if nothing had happened. I texted Stella and told her I'd be at the Enchanted a little late. I wasn't sure why I did that. She had no idea about anything that had happened anyway. Bessie let me know that Holiday Hills humans believed Gabe had returned from a specialized mission with the Georgia Bureau of Investigations, and that Remmington accepted a job in another state. As far as Stella knew, I had been out of town working on that manuscript, and I knew nothing, but I'd explained in my text that I'd heard everything from Gabe and Remmington, and I didn't want to talk about it.

I was desperate to see Gabe, but I was angry with him too. I called him and asked him to come by before I left to meet Stella.

Things were awkward between us. I wondered if they'd ever be what they were.

"So," he said. "You probably have some questions."

Cooper sat on the back of the chair and kept his eyes focused on Gabe. "One wrong move," he said, "and I'm all over that warlock."

I sat on the couch and pulled my knees to my chest. "You think?"

"Okay then. Go ahead. Ask me anything."

"It wasn't your brother in my dreams a few months ago, and you knew that, didn't you?"

"Yes."

"And you knew it was the real Dexius."

"I suspected, which is why I left. He'd somehow been released from prison, and I knew I had to find him. I knew he was coming for me, and that he'd get his revenge by hurting you."

"But he was here. You knew that."

"No, Abby. I didn't. Dexius is a powerful warlock. He cast a spell, so when I did see you with him, I saw an entirely different person with another name. I've been focused on finding Dexius looking like the mountain man, thinking he was hiding in the mountains."

"But the letter in your safe? Did you leave that for me?"

"I knew you were home then. Dexius had me all over Kentucky, Georgia, and Tennessee. We're still trying to figure it out. But yes, I left the letter. I'd even been in contact with Remmington, the real Remmington. I asked him to keep you safe. I didn't know at the time that Dexius was pretending to be him."

"I'm so confused."

"Don't be. It's all done now," he said. "Dexius, the mountain man, will never bother you again."

"How did your brother get involved?"

"Dexius did that when he told you the mountain man was my brother."

"Wouldn't you have known then that it was Dexius doing everything?"

"The spell, Abby. He'd changed everything for me. Think of how Stella and other humans see something human instead of magical whenever something magical happens. It's the same concept. Somehow Dexius's spell tricked me into seeing an alternate reality. The only thing I could see was your relationship with Remmington."

My heart dropped into my gut. "I thought you wanted me to move on."

"That was another one of Dexius's cruel jokes. He's always liked to push the limits."

"Is your brother evil?"

"Not even close."

"Why couldn't you tell me about Dexius or Jim for that matter? Why just make something up and leave like you did?"

"In retrospect I should have. I should have known you'd want to find me once you thought I was in danger." He took in a breath and let it out slowly. "And Jim? I've always worried I'd tell you something that could get you hurt, so I just didn't say much."

I bit my bottom lip. I had more questions, but I wasn't ready to ask them. I was ready to get back to normal, to have Gabe back in my life, though I wasn't sure in what way, and to hang out at the Enchanted and laugh at Mr. Charming. I just wanted my normal, magical life. "I have to apologize to Waylon."

He dipped his head to the side. "Waylon Hastings?"

"I heard you brought him in for questioning."

"Yes."

"Why? He said you two never had a confrontation."

"We didn't. I brought him in to kindly request he start treating others with respect. It wasn't a bad talk. It went well."

"Well, he's changed, but not because of you."

"One of Bessie's drink additions?"

"Nope. They're a couple."

His eyes widened. "Bessie and that cantankerous coot? Dating?" He shook his head. "I don't believe it."

"Things change."

"I know." He looked at Cooper and then back at me. "What about you? Do you still love me? Have you changed?"

In that moment, I knew. I knew he was the one. "I'm not all that interested in change."

EPILOGUE

It took some time, but things with Gabe went back to normal both at work, and with me. He busted the mayor for stealing from the city, and the town called him a hero.

Bessie and Waylon were the town's favorite couple, though all of Holiday Hills was still shocked at his transformation.

Stella and I did make it to the farmer's market. It felt good to hang out with my best friend and just be a girl. A witch girl, really.

∽

TWO WEEKS LATER, I awoke cranky and sad. Stella had informed me she had a job offer in New York City, and she was considering taking it. I couldn't imagine Holiday Hills without my best friend. I was happy for her. She was an excellent editor, and any company would be better with her, but I was sad for me. Talk about conflicted feelings.

Tobias Wheeler, a friendly shapeshifter I liked, called me. "Abby, we have a problem."

"What's wrong?" I asked, though I wasn't all that interested to find out.

"It's that reporter from the TV, Jessie Rosenblatt. I think she knows our secret."

"Secret?"

"She knows we're magical, and she's threatening to tell the world."

Purchase Bust a Witch here to find out what happens next!

ALSO BY CAROLYN RIDDER ASPENSON

The Rachel Ryder Thriller Series

The Lily Sprayberry Cozy Mystery Series

The Midlife in Castleberry Paranormal Cozy Mystery Series

The Pooch Party Cozy Mystery Series

The Witches of Holiday Hills Cozy Mystery Series

The Midlife Psychic Medium Series

Formerly The Angela Panther Mystery Series

The Magical Real Estate Mystery Series

Other Books

Mourning Crisis

Join Carolyn's Newsletter List and receive special downloads, sales, and other exciting authory things here.

ABOUT THE AUTHOR

USA Today Bestselling Author Carolyn Ridder Aspenson writes cozy mysteries, thrillers, and paranormal women's fiction featuring strong female leads. Her stories shine through her dialogue, which readers have praised for being realistic and compelling.

Her first novel, Unfinished Business, was a five-star Reader's Favorite, a Rone Award finalist, and a number one bestseller on both Amazon and Barnes and Noble. In 2021, she introduced readers to detective Rachel Ryder in Damaging Secrets. Overkill, the third book in the Rachel Ryder series, was one of Thrillerfix's best thrillers of 2021.Reviews have praised her work as *'compelling, and intense,'* and *'read through the night, edge of your seat thrillers'*.

Prior to publishing, she worked as a journalist in the suburbs of Atlanta where her work appeared in multiple newspapers and magazines. She wrote a monthly featured column in Northside Woman magazine.

Writing is only one of Carolyn's passions. She is an avid dog lover and currently spoils two pit bull boxer mixes. She lives in the mountains of North Georgia as an empty nester with her husband, a cantankerous cat, and those two spoiled dogs. You can chat with Carolyn on Facebook at Carolyn Ridder Aspenson Books or through her website at www.carolynridderaspenson.com

Made in the USA
Monee, IL
20 March 2023